Leg of Jane

Welcome To Satanville, Volume 1

Jimi Peranteau

Published by Jimi Peranteau, 2023.

LEG OF JANE

First edition. January 25, 2023.

Copyright © 2023 Jimi Peranteau.

ISBN: 979-8215226315

Written by Jimi Peranteau.

Also by Jimi Peranteau

Welcome To Satanville
Leg of Jane
Bloodlines

Watch for more at https://www.amazon.com/author/jimperanteau_13.

This book is dedicated to my dad, who is always telling me that I'm a writer, and I should write a nice love story....well I guess I should work a little harder on the "love" aspect of it huh?

Also to my best friend J. My brother in music who sat with me and said "sure, lets write a movie"... okay, so it's not a movie, but I think it's better this way.

Finally to my beautiful wife, who read each chapter as I wrote it, had to listen to all my weird little ideas and somehow still put up with me.

I love you all, and this,... this if for you.

Chapter 1

We've all heard the stories. At least once. I can still hear the warnings my parents would give me every time we drove by that god forsaken road. I can still remember how my mother would say, "Now Janey, don't you ever find yourself down that road. Bad people live down there." Maybe it was because of her always having to push it into my brain that caused me to be so curious. Or maybe it was just my imagination running wild each time we would drive by. Either way, I would always stare through my window, trying to see down that pitch black road.

Back then, I never could figure out what could have been so bad about those people. Just the simple question of who these people were would send my mind into a frenzy. It appeared as though she had always made them out to be what nightmares are truly made of. What was so terrible that my mother would warn me to stay away from even the road itself? The road! I mean...

It was just a road after all... wasn't it?

Despite that, in those moments, it seemed to have been working. My fear of what may lie down that road was overpowering my curiosity. Even as I would press my face against the cold car window, I would say aloud, "but it's just a road.. what's so bad about that road?"

Once my curiosity filled daydreams would subside, I would find myself back in my seat. My father's eyes fixated on me through the rear-view mirror. His brow was stern, but his darkened eyes would quickly lighten up. Next, as always, he would give me a little wink, and his eyes would return to the road. Eventually, he would turn the radio up; instantly my curiosity would move to the songs.

That's how it went, every day until the sixth grade. I can still remember it clearly. Very clearly. It was the day that all of my mother's warnings had finally made sense. When they were no longer just stories and empty instructions. That was the day they found that poor girl. Everything around me seemed to come to a halting stop. I think that was the first time I ever experienced a complete tunnel vision. If you have ever experienced tunnel vision out of sheer fear, then you can understand. It's as though nothing else even matters.

I had just walked through the door, and what had seemed to be the perfect day quickly began to no longer matter. I could hear the television in the family room; it was awfully loud. My dad wouldn't even have it that loud for the big game. Which, I'm sure, is why I remember the volume of it. "Go to your room Janey," my father strictly demanded of me. "But I just got home, and I'm thirsty." I paused and gave a quick glance from around the corner as I hung my backpack on the wooden coat rack that was kept by the front door. Looking back, I remember hoping that he was not paying too much attention to me. "I'm hungry too. What do we have to-"

"Now Jane! I'll bring you something in a few minutes. You really don't need to be seeing this." When my father interrupted, you knew he was serious. Of all the things he despised, out of all the points he would teach me never to do during a conversation; interruption was number one! But I was almost a teenager, and being almost a teen means almost doing what you are told. And I wanted to see what all the fuss was about. What was on the news that I really don't need to be seeing? That's when I realized that my day no longer mattered. At least, not to me anyway.

The headline was simple, but effective. It read: Unidentified body has local police concerned. When the reporter said the location, I immediately remembered every single warning my mother had given to me. Every moment of fear and confusion came rushing back like an icy shiver sprinting down the length of

my spine. At that moment, it was no longer just some story people would tell trying to make you cringe. Every last now Janey hit me like a brick wall. It was so overwhelming that I had completely missed the entire conversation whispered between my parents.

Honestly though, I don't think I really cared what m parents were talking about. I'm sure the whispering was their way of protecting me from something as terrible as murder; but I was more interested in what the news was saying.

My father had channel six on in the living room. The kitchen television was tuned to channel three, and the den was tuned into channel twenty nine. All the stations seemed to show the same views, and each one had the same information. Absolutely nothing.

It was easy to see the tension that was building up, and I'm pretty sure that was exactly the reason the field reporter had finally decided to sneak past everyone that had been blocking the road. Because of this, he had burned a moment into my memory that I will never forget. One that I am certain, so many other people share with me. Even his name was etched in... Mathew Lansing.

I swear I'll never forget that name.

"And we're back from a quick break. I'm Monica Brackson, and if you are just tuning in, we are ready to go live on scene with Action News field reporter Matt Lansing in Chadds Ford, Pennsylvania where a terrible tragedy has occurred. We are not being told much more that a body has been discovered. Matt, it looks like there is quite a bit of commotion happening over there. Is there anything you can tell us? Have you managed to get anyone to talk to you?"

"Monica, at this time, all we are being told is that the body of a young female has been discovered. I have tried repeatedly to get some kind of interview started with police officers. At the very least, a simple question answered. Unfortunately, no one is talking at this time. None of the reporters here are quite sure why there is so much silence. My guess is the brutal nature of the crime." The confusion on Monica's face was obvious. "I'm sorry, you just said brutal. Have you heard something new? We're pretty much in the dark over here."

"Well, I'm pretty much as informed as you guys in the station are, but what I am gathering is that what has happened here is unimaginable, and brutal, to say the least. Earlier, I overheard one officer say that this was the most disgusting act of violence. Just a few moments ago, I was able to hear a conversation between a few officers. One of whom had stated the individual responsible must be bitter and heartless, extremely disturbed, and without a conscious; let alone remorse. But as you can see, we are being kept at a distance from that actual crime scene."

I don't know how he was able to stay so calm. Not even the police officers could keep themselves together. Apparently, the police had no plans to be dealing with this alone. They called in the Federal Bureau of Investigation. It appeared as though the whole agency had come to our town.

Most of the news stations only showed the overpowering blue and red lights from the vehicles that were blocking the road. All the reporters had set up on Baltimore Pike, right in front of the big black SUV's and the long black sedans of the FBI. Every last one of them was eagerly waiting for any kind of statement from anyone who was willing to talk.

Everyone wanted something more than the usual reports of: we may have an experienced killer, possibly even a serial killer on the loose, that the news had been saying for what seemed to be hours. Unfortunately, no one was allowed to get anywhere close to the scene, and no one was talking. They used their vehicles and the local police cars to make sure no reporters made it through; well, all but one.

Mr. Lansing had managed to sneak past everyone through the woods that surrounded the area. My guess is that he was familiar with the area, but I can not be certain. Honestly, I never really cared enough to find out, but anyway. He got himself real close. Maybe too close. I remember seeing the lights from the cars, all the cops walking around holding their stomachs. Even the big guys were having troubles of their own.

Then came the view I remember the most. Even now, it still runs a frigid chill down my spine.

Oh, that poor girl.

The camera man didn't realize what he had just shown the world. Not at first. When he had finally realized what he was filming, he flashed the camera away, pointing it directly at the ground. Oh, but it was too late.

She was bound to a large tree. Someone had tightly pulled her arms back. Her hands looked as though she had been grabbing at the tree bark in some kind of desperate attempt to relieve the pain of each of her hands being nailed to it. Her legs each had several large old rail spikes in them; starting from just below the hips and reaching as far down as her ankles. Making the securing of her to the tree complete. Her genitals had been removed, leaving a gaping hole where her uterus and colon appeared to be pulled through. Both of her breast had been cut clean off, almost as though it was a careful procedure. It was obvious that whoever did this wanted the breast to remain as a single intact piece. The word whore had been carved into her stomach. An old wooden bat riddled with rusted over concrete nails had been left violently lodged in her face. The bat, horizontal in its placement, looked as if the force of the swings had nearly split the bat in two. The base of the tree soaked in blood, and an ax still laid embedded deep within her abdomen, as though it was underlining the title of whore that had been given to her.

For weeks, the murder was on the news. Eventually, she had been identified, but the headlines always read the same: Authorities still baffled in Chadds Ford murder. And: Still no leads in the murder of Marcie Richmond. For years, it went unsolved. Inevitably, it went cold. Finally, it would be filled away and was forgotten by most.

But not us.

Chapter 2

Jake and I have been friends since the third grade. We consistently managed to get ourselves into trouble going places we had not allowed in. So, in the end, I suppose it comes as no shock to anyone we would end up finding ourselves in this position together.

Jake always had been a serious prankster. He loved a good joke, and consistently devising his next big one. It's what made him the happiest. You and I may find Christmas or Thanksgiving as our favorite holiday, Jake, his is April fool's day. Well, if I am being perfectly honest, it was more like April fool's month. It had never been just a one day event with him. That just wouldn't be sufficient. "You can blame me," Jake would say. "I was raised this way!" He swore he picked it up from his old man, and believe me, if you ever met the guy, you would understand. Heaven help you if you ended up in the same room with the two of them, especially in April!

Truthfully, I guess I would be lying if I said that I didn't enjoy the pranks. Yeah, they were fun. I'll give him that much. And yes, at times, they could be a bit overboard, but despite that, they were always harmless fun. There was this one time he had brought a homemade stink-bomb into school. I put myself on the lookout as he poured it onto the music teacher's seat. I tried so hard not to laugh hysterically when she decided it was pop quiz day. Quiet chuckles permeated the room as she went up and down the aisles, handing out the quiz papers. The rest of the school year, the kids referred to that day as the poop quiz day!

God, I will never forget that smell!

That was our life. We were proud of it, and everyone knew it. I did my fair share of helping with his pranks. Even had a hand in working out a few of them out. By the third year of high school, there wasn't a single person left for Jake to joke with. Not the principal, not the cafeteria workers. Hell, not even the janitor found himself safe from Jake's practical jokes. There was literally no one left in the school for Jake to prank.

Until she came.

Rachel had transferred to our school in the middle of eleventh grade. She was shy and kept to herself in the beginning. You know how they say your first impression is the most important? Well, hers was that of a bookworm. She didn't seem to want to know who anyone was, always keeping her face buried deep inside her books. But Jake made sure she knew explicitly who he was. She learned early on that Jake was a jokester. Regrettably, she found that out the hard way.

It was Rachel's second week in, and she found herself unable to locate one of her classes. Instinctively, she asked the first person she could get to stop long enough to ask for help, which, of course, was Jake. He advised her to take the west wing stairs to the third floor. It would be the last door on the left. What she found was the girls' room on a floor that was no longer being used. Ultimately, she found the right room, and the first person she sees as she enters is Jake; settled right near the door. The grin on his face reached proudly from one ear to the other.

It didn't take her long to make friends, though. She found her way into our little click; I guess you would call it that. There weren't many of us, but most of us stayed close to each other during those years. We were clearly not the nerdy kids, and nowhere near the jocks. We didn't get along with those kids. It's not like it was anything personal. We just didn't want to associate with the kind of people who would make it a point to go out of their way to push the little guy down. I guess I never quite figured out the satisfaction of cramming someone inside of a locker.

Besides, we were happy enough with our limited group of friends. There was me, Jake, Mike, Rachel, Chris, Luke, Reen and Worm. And please, don't ask how he picked up that name.

Jake and I always spent more of our time away from school with Mike and Rachel, rather than with the other guys. If I had to pin down the reasoning behind that, well then, I guess it would really come down to two reasons.

First, and presumably, the most obvious, distance. It was not like we all lived on the same block. Let alone neighborhood. In our area, you would live miles apart and attend the same school. Rachel and Mike, they lived closer to me, as well as Jake.

The second, well, while we were friends, yes, we differed from each other. Almost entirely. Some of the same interests, yes, but that was pretty much it. The best way to explain it would be that we had different ethics. We wanted more out of our lives, to make something of ourselves, while those guys pretty much just wanted to float through life; one party after another. And the four of us, we could only handle small doses of the guys. Honestly, I'm sure I could say the same for them.

Rachel got close to Mike in the twelfth grade. Which had made her much more accessible to Jake and his pranks. You see, Mike and Jake, they were good friends, and close. They had been inseparable since kindergarten. I guess that's what happens when you're neighbors.

Jake and Mike grew up together, so interests in things like movies, television, video games and outdoor activities were all the same. However, it's their future interests that differed between the two of them, as well as interests in women. Either way, they bonded closer than most brothers do.

After high school is when we all separated from each other. Most of us went on to hold jobs, trying to pay our way through college. Mike worked as a transport tech at the local hospital. It was good money and kept him around the field he was in schooling for. Rachel followed right behind him. She wanted to be a nurse while his plans focused on the forensic sciences field. So Mike got her a job with him.

Jake went on to work on vehicles. He wasn't overly interested in college. He always said the extra schooling really wasn't for him. He was pretty good at it, too. Jake always had a knack for vehicles. Their engines, body work, electrical, the whole nine yards really. It was almost a second nature to him. Like he knew instinctively what went where, how all the little thing would work together. Everything. Me, I was proud of him. He knew exactly what he wanted out of life, and the way I see it, why waste away trying to do something that you're not passionate about, or even good at?

Me, I was never interested in college either. Twelve years of school had been enough for me. I decided in my early teen years that I was going to be a radio DJ. I figured a few months of training and I could grab an internship at one of the local radio stations. Work my way up from there. Let me tell you, man, was I wrong about the training! Definitely a lot longer than a few months of training. So, I took a course in communications and broadcasting and got myself a gig at a radio station not too far from my house. The station was called y100. It was a nice little spot. Paid little, but that didn't bother me. It was the experience that mattered to me. Really broke my heart when they shut down.

Luke and Reen both ended up working at Burger King. We figured out quickly that those two, would never amount to much of anything. Luke followed Reen around like a lost puppy and believed everything he said. But not us. We knew not to believe what came out of his mouth. Which is probably the biggest reason we stopped hanging around him. During school years was one thing, but after we graduated and moved on, we looked at it like this: when you can't believe what someone says, then trust is nonexistent. When you can't trust someone, why place yourself in that kind of predicament?

As for Chris and Worm, they became drug dealers. Never any of the serious stuff, just pot and a few pain pills every now and then. Chris got the normal stuff, nothing real fancy, but Worm, he got the good stuff. And he knew it.

We all liked to smoke pot. Never really found anything bad about it. Sure, we drank and smoked, but as long as the bills got paid, then we were all right. That's how we saw it. Perhaps that's the only reason we still talked to Chris and Worm. Never really wanted to get our stuff from some guy on a corner. That never seemed safe to us. Looking back at it today, they would still be here if we didn't call them that night.

Chapter 3

We had been planning for months with this party. It was going to be a great time. A little booze, some pot, kick ass music, and the biggest prank me and Jake had ever pulled off. A friend of mine was going to help us out big time. His name was Josh. He was a good guy, and fun to be around. I met him at the radio station I worked at. Josh was another intern trying to work his way up. We got along great and he loved Jake's pranks. The whole joke was going to be directed at Rachel, and Mike's job was to make sure she came. Getting him to go along with it was a complete job altogether. So Jake took care of that part.

"C'mon dude, it's nothing but a little prank. No one is going to get hurt. Besides, she brought it on herself when she said I'll never pull another joke on her." Jake told Mike while pushing his elbow into his arm. "I don't know man. Is it worth all the trouble you and Jane are going through? You know Rachel's always watching out for you." Mike responded. "What happens if it doesn't work out, you know, like you're expecting? Suddenly it's all a complete waste of time, and you spend months swearing and working out another way to pull one of your jokes on her."

"Look Mike, if it doesn't work out, it doesn't work out! We still got a killer party in the middle of the cemetery. Lots of booze, good friends and loud music!" Jake patted Mike's back, trying to reassure him that everything would work out as planned.

"Yeah, and let's talk about the location dude. Of all places you pick that place. Satanville!" Turning to Jake and grabbing his shoulder, Mike's voice became stern and serious. "I remember what happened there. Hell, I know damn well you and Jane remember." Jake immediately interrupts, "Dude, that was how many years ago? Not a damn thing has happened since then." He leads Mike over to the time clock. "Just don't worry about it. You get Rachel and the beer and swing by my place and get me. You do this, and I'll call Worm and get some of the good shit for after I scare the shit out of her!"

Mike clocks out of work and looks at Jake, nudging him.

Now with his index finger pointing at the center of Jake's chest, he says with a relatively serious tone in his voice, "dude this,.. this better be worth it. And you better not fuck things up for me with her. Alright?" Jake didn't need to respond. The expression on his face said everything. It was that unmistakable 'just stop stalling already. We all know the both of you can't get enough of each other' look.

"Okay," Mike went on, "I pick up the beer, Rachel and you, but how is Jane getting there?" Jake responds with a grin growing on his face, "Josh is taking care of that one. They should be getting ready right now. I'll meet you at my place, two hours, no more. Don't forget, make sure your ass calls me to let me know Rachel isn't chickening out."

"Whatever dude, tonight better be good." Slamming his car door shut, he heard Jake yell out...

"It's to die for!"

Chapter 4

I can recall the thrill on Josh's face as he was helping me get ready. Eyes wide with excitement, one hell of a smile across his face. Josh was eager to see the finished results. He loved Halloween, everything about it, most of all, making people look as scary as possible. As for me, I loved to terrify people.

So there I was, getting all decked out to look like that poor girl they had found so many years ago. I had some good ol' Mudvayne blaring throughout my apartment. Their second album is a favorite for me, 'The end of all things to come'. I could listen to the song Solve Et Coagula on repeat for hours. Come to think of it, I believe that was the song that was on when we finished getting me ready. My face looked horrifying. Dried blood, fresh blood, it was all there. My face looked like someone had violently beaten it in with a nailed bat. I had taken an old outfit, one I had barely worn anymore, and rolled it around in the dirt, making it look old and ragged. I cut the bottom half of the shirt off and ripped up the skirt a bit.

Jake stopped by to check on the progress of, well, me. As he arrived, Josh had just finished the makeup on my stomach, pale skin, and of course, whore across my stomach. I opened the door to see Jake looking thoroughly horrified. "Your just now getting up?" He asked me. Obviously, I knew he was being sarcastic, but I told him to shut the hell up anyway! I then proceeded to give a little spin, showing off the incredible job Josh had done with my makeup.

Josh came out from the kitchen in a hurry. "Yo dude!" His voice filled with excitement, "check it out man, she's dead!" His arms outstretched in my direction in a bit of a presenting manor. I gave another quick spin, and struck a slight pose, moving my hands down the lent of my body, but Jake shrugged his shoulders while saying "yeah, but you didn't need to do all that makeup. She looks horrible enough without it." There was a slight chuckle in his voice as he looked at me and gave me a little wink with his right eye. "Hey now asshole, I'm right here you know." I shouted, stepping up to him, grabbing his shirt and balling it up within my fist. "Keep it up and watch what happens!"

See, Jake had no idea what was in store for him. He always thought that he was the best jokester. No one could ever pull a fast one on him. He would always say, "you can't prank a prankster." But he would find out just how wrong he was soon enough.

Because of my curiosity about how capable we were of accomplishing this, Josh and I ran over the details as Jake's phone rang. The idea, that was mine, and it was brilliant! Scare the guy who spent most of his life joking around and scaring everyone else while he's too busy with his own little scheme. But this brought it to two simultaneous pranks on two separate people. Knowing Josh wanted a chance at pulling a prank on Jake, he did the planning. Because of this, I was more in the dark about it than Jake.

Josh explained it as secretly as he could while Jake was on the phone with Mike. "See, I informed him it would be better if he went with Mikey and Rachel." He explained in a whisper while hiding a brief peek over his shoulder at Jake. "Told him it's less suspicious if he is with Rachel. This way, she's not expecting another one of his little jokes." He continued, "but we will be swinging by my buddy's house and grabbing him along the way." Josh gave another glance in Jake's direction, just in time to see him finishing up his phone call. "When we show up," he finished quickly, "he'll go around back of the cemetery while we pull in the front. Jake will be too busy looking for us and never expect what's coming."

Jake came storming into the kitchen with his face all lit up. I knew that face. That's the same look he gets every time one of his plans comes together. "Alright, I gotta roll," he said, eyes wide with anticipation. "Mike will be at my place within an hour. I'm trusting you guys with this, so don't fuck it up!" He ran out of my apartment more excited than I had ever seen him before. He had no idea what was coming.

-But really, None of us knew what was going to happen-

Chapter 5

Mike had reached at Jake's house right when he stated he would. He was always a punctual guy. If he said an hour, he meant an hour. And, of course, Jake was ready to go.

I'll never know how he maintained a straight face. You could always tell when he was excited, and even more so when he was overly excited. He would get this big grin on his face, clearly would not make a good poker player! Later in the evening, he told me all the details of their ride to Satanville, so I guess being in the back seat of Mike's car helped out a lot. I will say I was interested in knowing what the ride in was like. So I was all ears as he filled in the details-

"So what's the story with this place anyway? What's so scary about a little old graveyard?" Rachel asks as she lit a small pipe packed neatly with marijuana, taking in a big drag. Trying to hold her breath in the best she can, she continued, "so what if the headstones all have the same last name? Some families just want to be buried with each other." She coughs while finally exhaling. She gently pats on her chest, hoping to ease the coughing and hands the bowl to Jake. "Its not just the cemetery," Mike tells her. "There's an entire story to the place. It happened about twenty years ago." Jake interrupted Mike, eager to tell the story. "Dude, let me tell the story. You'll mess it up, like always."

Mike, holding the smoke in his lungs, says "bullshit man, I'm just as capable of telling it as you!" Jake laughs and corrects Mike. "Dude, no. Hand me the bowl; shut up and listen." Jake had told the story of Chadds Fords' very own Bean family plenty of times. He knew it like the back of his hand. He always seemed to be the guy that all our new residents would go to when they wanted to learn about Satanville.

"Ok Rach, listen up." He takes a deep hit from the pipe, hands it to Rachel, and continues on. "It's said that one family lives back here and owns all the land. They are a rich inbred family, and get this, best of all, they're all Satan worshipers. Every so often, one of their children will be born deformed. So, in belief that they had angered Satan, instead of understanding what the potential affects of in-breeding are; they would sacrifice the newborn, offering it to their god."

"Wait," Rachel interrupted, "is this true? You know, the whole,.. inbred satanic family thing? Don't other people live back there? You don't really expect me to believe that everyone back there, are all Satan worshiping in-breeders, do you?" Rachel was laughing, clearly not falling for Jake's story of the Beans. But Jake, he did not miss a beat. Confident in himself, he explained, "obviously not everyone in the area, are Beans. Money does eventually run out, you know this. Income must come in regardless of how much you have. Story is they own the entire area and rent it out to everyone who lives back there. They keep a large portion of land for themselves, and part of the rental conditions is to stay off their property." Rachel nodded her head in agreement, and Jake knew he had her right where he wanted her.

"Where was I?" Jake questioned himself as he tried to continue his story. "Oh yeah, sacrificed baby, that's right!" He took a final drag from the pipe after pausing. "They would take the remains of the child, wrap it in cloth and shove it inside this old tree. The trees that grow across from it are crazy. Not straight up like a tree should grow, but would bend in the middle, ninety degrees away from the sacrifice tree."

"I call bullshit!" Rachel proclaimed, "trees grow towards the sun, including bending in order to receive a greater amount of sunlight. Did you not pay attention in science class?" Mike responded quickly, "Not on flat ground they don't! You'll see soon enough. There's no over-crowding, no steep hill inclines. No reasonable explanation for the bending. Besides, it's the only place they bend, and the farther away from the sacrifice tree, the less they bend."

Jake took back control of the conversation, quite impressed by Mike's explanation. "It was always said not to go in these areas. Our parents would tell us bad people live back there. We never knew what they meant, never really believed the warnings. Until twenty years ago. They found a girl tied and nailed to that old tree. Her body was mangled, beaten, and bloody. They never found her killers, but we all knew who did it. It was the Beans." Interrupting Jake's story, Rachel asks "the Beans? So they're killers too?" Jake leans in closer to the front seat, and answers, "that's what I've been saying Rach! I'm just trying to tell you the story!" The car slows down as they turn a corner and climb the road, entering Satanville. "But anyway," Jake continues, "every year on the anniversary of the girl's death, her ghost comes back to this road. It's said, if you get out of your car and wait around, she will grab you, screaming about taking her home. Then, no matter where you are back here, she will drag you to the tree where she kills you."

The car comes to a stop and Rachel looks out her window to see the bent trees. Mike grabs her shoulder and points out his window. "That's the old tree right there. They filled it with cement after they found her remains." Rachel, shocked, looks at the tree and asks, "When's this anniversary anyway?" Jake places his hand on her shoulder, looks her straight in the eyes, never blinking and tells her,

"Tonight"

Chapter 6

We arrived at the cemetery about half an hour after Jake and Mike arrived. Jake sent me a text asking where we were. I replied to it by telling him we got held up trying to get a hold of Chris. He was still clueless about the actual plan. Josh's friend lived across town, near the mall. So it took longer than I expected, and Josh, he's always pretty good at leaving out details like that; but we made good time on the way back.

His friend didn't say much, not even his name. Which, if I am being honest, kind of creeped me out. Josh reassured me that everything would be fine. His exact words were: "Look, he's only shy until he gets a few drinks in him. So, chill out Jane, everything's gonna be fine."

I didn't care about that. All I knew was, he's not someone that I wanted to spend time alone with. Nor did I plan to. First impressions are important to me. His, well, let's just say it was less than impressionable. Far less.

When we arrived at the graveyard, we had parked out of sight, on the only shoulder of the road. It was my first time in the area, and it was very dark. So naturally, I had no idea where I was. On the other hand, Josh had been here several times and knew precisely where he was. I guess his parents didn't give him the same warnings my parents had given me. Mr. Shy had run off into the trees, vanishing into the darkness.

I was relieved to be away from him, finally. Josh could tell I wasn't too sure about the guy. He knew I was always the type of person who followed their gut feelings, but he reassured me once again that I need to give Mr. Shy another chance, and I needed to give people more than just that first impression.

I had just finished sending Jake a text message that read 'we are here' when we came up to the edge of the cemetery. We stayed at the edge of the tree line, waiting for the right moment to 'strike'. We had the perfect view of them. For us, they were in plain sight. However, they could not see us at all. The music was loud enough to hear from my position. What they were listening to surprised me.

It was heavy, really heavy. I had always been into rock music, but once high school came around, I found myself listening to more of the metal genre. The louder the better! The sound of the guitars screaming through the speakers, the speed of the drums, the crunching bass. It all intrigued me. I found myself getting lost in my amazement at their choice of music when Josh nudged me on my arm. He took off running across the field along the edge of the road. By the time Rachel had noticed him, he had reached the other side and disappeared into the trees. I could hear Rachel from where I was standing.

"What the hell was that?" She said, standing up, trying to see what had run across the field. "I don't know what you're talking 'bout," Jake replied. "I saw something run across the field." She looks at Mike for support. "I don't know either, Rach. I wasn't paying any attention." Josh takes off running again. This time he heads back towards me while Rachel is talking to Mike. He made it only part way across before turning back. This time, Rachel got a clear sight of him as he reached the tree line.

Not sure of what she had just seen, her scream lasted for only a quick second. "Right there!" she yelled out. "I just seen it again! Go check it out, Jake." I tried hard not to laugh. "No way!" Jake responded, trying to sound startled. "I'm not going alone. You're coming with me." He told her. "No fucking way Jake, take Mike with you." she tells him, pushing Mike forward. "Don't look at me!" Mike told Rachel, "You can just leave me outta this one!"

Jake, looking at Rachel, finally spoke up, "You're the one that keeps seeing something. Now I can go with you, if you want, or you can go by yourself. It's your choice." Rachel looks at Jake and agrees. "Fine," she said, reluctantly, "but you're in front."

Alright, I thought to myself. Now it's my turn. I ran over the plan one last time. I was sure I was good to go. Now it's time to scare this girl big time, but first I had to wait, wait for Jake to get what's coming for him! I don't remember what I was more excited about, finally getting to pull a prank on Jake, or scaring the hell out of Rachel. Either way, I was about to find out.

Jake led the way, staying close to the tree line. Rachel stayed right behind him, looking back every few seconds to make sure Mike was watching out for them. And that's when it happened. While she was turned facing Mike, Mr. Shy leans out of the woods grabbing Jake and pulling him into the trees. The sound of Jake screaming in shock got Rachel's attention. She turned back just in time to see Jake being pulled through the trees. His feet dragging across the dirt, his arms above his head, as his screams filled the woods. This must have really freaked her out. She took off running, straight towards me.

I waited until she got close and jumped out. I ran straight for her. My arms stretched out, hands open and yelling, help me! When she saw me, she stopped dead in her tracks. Every ounce of tone faded from her face. Her jaw dropped open, eyes wide. If the hair on her head could stand on end, believe me, it would have. She turned and tried to get back to Mike, but it was too late. I grabbed both her arms and started saying take me home!

Gradually I got louder and louder until I was screaming. By now, I had noticed Jake coming out of the trees, laughing hysterically. Rachel had fallen to her knees, trying to free herself. I never heard her curse before tonight, but she let out the mother of all curses. As she hit the ground, she blurted out, oh fuck! The position she put herself in, I called an audible. I pulled her backwards onto the dirt, dragged her backwards a short distance and said sternly once more, take me home! That's about the time when she looked at my face and said, "Jane?" I couldn't hold it in anymore. I cracked up. I laughed so hard I fell to the ground, holding my stomach.

Rachel stood up while yelling, "Dicks! Your all dicks! Every one of you, except for her. She's a fucking cunt! Fucking dicks!" And that's when the party started.

We all sat down next to a small fire-pit and sparked up a bowl. Good ol' fire-pit pot circle, as Jake put it. Mike handed each of us a beer as he said, "Well, sure was about damn time someone gave Jake a taste of his own medicine. Mr. you can't prank a prankster." The joy on Mike's face could have lit that entire cemetery.

Mike sat down next to Rachel, looked at Jake with a grin from ear to ear. "So," he asked, "how's it feel to have the shit scared out of you?" Jake laughed, "dude you knew about this, didn't you?" Jake asked Mike, almost certain he knew the answer. "Not a clue man," he responded, "but I wish I did! You should have heard yourself. You sounded like a little girl!"

Jake gave a short ha ha and took a sip of his beer. "And who is this guy that grabbed me, anyway?" He asked. And that was the first time I heard Mr. Shy speak. "Well, she's been calling me Mr. Shy, I kind of like that, but my name is Dan." He replied while pointing at me.

"Well, maybe if you said at least something, even just made yourself noticed," I told Dan, "I would have given you a different name." Dan looked at me with his head tilted down. "Oh, is that so?" he asked me. "Absolutely," I said, as I slowly felt more comfortable around him. "Maybe even something like Mr. Dude that's gonna make Jake shit his pants!" That made everyone laugh for a bit. Until we realized we just smoked our last bowl.

Mike and Rachel were talking when I made the announcement. "Hey guys, no more pot," Mike quickly tossed Jake his phone. "You owe me a bag of Worms." I could tell Dan was a bit confused. "A bag of worms? I'll have to pass on that one." I laughed at his comment. "Worm is a friend from high school. He sells, but only top-notch shit. Trust me, you won't be disappointed." I told him.

Jake handed Mike his phone back and sat down next to me. "Worms not too far away, says he'll be here in 10 minutes." He was laughing as he told us this. "Yeah, but we know Worm," I said, laughing myself. "It'll take him about an hour before he gets here. His not too far away is across Philly." I continued on, reminding him of the last time we called on Worm. "It took him 45 minutes to go down the road last month." Jake moved closer to me and handed me another beer. "Don't worry," he said, "I called Chris too. He should be here shortly. I told him to hang out for a while, too. He sounded pretty excited. Time with the old gang would benefit us all. Now here, drink, damn it."

"Your trying to get me drunk, aren't you?" I asked as I opened the beer. "Hey what can I say?" He had a quirky little smile as he continued on. "Look at you, with your long red hair, those light gray eyes. Not too tall, and always with an all natural face." He released a handful of my hair as he ran his fingers down the length of it and continued on with the compliments. "No lipstick, eye shadow or any makeup. Well, except tonight, but that's okay; it's understandable. And you know how I am. I'm a sucker for a redhead. You should have known better when you dyed your hair red." I leaned back and squinted my eyes. "Really? Should have known better, huh? Is that so?" I was sarcastic, but he knew that. "Sometimes I swear you do these things on purpose."

I smiled as I took a sip of my beer. "That's not how you were acting earlier tonight. Pretty sure you called me ugly." When I said that, I winked, because I knew very well how Jake felt about me. I never could understand it.

I never thought of myself as attractive. I was never the real skinny type. There was some meat on my bones, which, as most girls would, had a bit of a complex about it. But that didn't bother Jake. Even though we always would say things to each other that would end most friendships, we were only joking around; and we both knew it.

During our time in middle school, we became more than just friends. And it stayed that way through all of high school. Everyone knew it too. Jake was a bit of the protective, jealous type when it came to me. If a new kid came to school after he was done with the initial joke, he would make sure they knew we were dating. He even did it to the girls, too! But now we were just friends again. I don't think he wanted it that way, but that didn't bother our friendship at all. He would always tell me we would end up back together one day, so he was just waiting for his day.

My parents were always fond of Jake. They would joke around and say things like, "hey, at least he's not family!". They were weird like that, but I loved them anyway. Their disappointment was obvious when I told them we had broken up. Maybe more upset than I was; it was kind of weird.

The party was going great. There was plenty of beer left to go around, and I had my music set at random, so I didn't need to watch over it constantly. Turned out that Josh was right about Dan. Once he got a few drinks in him, he completely opened up. He seemed like a decent enough guy. He didn't smoke though, which I guess that's also good. I asked him why, and he said his work does random drug test. Definitely a good reason not to smoke.

"Hey man, I guess I should be saying sorry." I told him. He looked at me, confused, like he had no idea why I was apologizing. Josh jumped in and let him in on how I was. "She's a bit picky with the people she meets." He explained. "Her parents always taught her to judge a person by their first impression, and if that first impression was one that stirred her gut, stay away from the guy."

"Hey its helped out so far," I defended myself. "Yeah, but it's not always fair. You can't just judge someone on the way they act the first time they meet you. You're an intimidating girl, you know. Thankfully, I was warned ahead of time to give you the best impression of me when I first met you." I laughed at him and said, "well you did pretty good, but you can't blame me for the way I was raised."

My attention was suddenly diverted when I saw the headlights pull up to the cemetery. It was Chris. "Well, it's about time!" Jake had said while he jumped up from the ground. The excitement quickly left as we saw who had just arrived. "Well, now we know what he meant by time with the old gang. I can't believe he brought Reen here." I said, shocked that Chris would even do something like this. "Oh, what the hell!" I heard Mike yell out as he was coming back from showing the headstones to Rachel.

"And yup, nothings changed. Still got his head shoved firmly up Reen's ass!" Mike had continued as Luke jumped out of the bed of Chris' truck. "Wow, I'm surprised the two of them weren't sitting on each other's laps," Rachel added. "Hey Dan," I said. "Believe nothing, the guy in the spiked hat says. Just take it with a grain of salt."

As the three of them headed over, I could see Jake tensing up. His foot tapped, his fingers tapping too, kind of like mimicking the drums on his leg. He would let out a few sighs here and there, and I swear, I could hear his teeth grinding away. Jake had a problem with Reen. Big time. A bit more than the rest of us. But that's a story for some other time.

I stood up and grasped Jake's arm, telling him, "just calm down and keep the peace like you've been doing." But I knew there was only so much anyone could take of that guy. Especially Jake. It was clear this night was going to get terrible sooner or later.

Chapter 7

Reen's arms raised high above his head as he shouted, "Hey, hey! Now this party can get started. I, am, here!" I shrugged my head as he started making his way around to everyone. To my surprise, everyone was being really nice to him. Even Jake kept his cool and shook his hand. "Where's the beer?" he asked. "I could use a cold one right now. Yo, last night, I was at this chick's house right,.." he babbled on, "getting drunk, fucking wasted bro, me and her, pounding down cold ones while her husband was at work." He smacked Jake on the shoulder, oblivious to the tension that had built up within him. "I drank like a case and a half by myself. Then I took care of her right in the bathroom cause I was throwing up a bit. Yeah, I'm a freak like that cause I'm the man. I am awesome!"

I looked at him a little cockeyed, "no," I said, "you're not awesome, you're just full of yourself, but let me know as soon as her husband finds out cause that I would love to see." His response was as typical as it can get for him. "Oh, I'm not worried about that, he's ok with it. And besides, if he tried anything on me, I'll just kick his ass cause I'm like a 22nd degree black belt in Tye Kwan Doe. Plus, I'm a master of Ju Jitz Zu. I call it Tye Kwan Jitz Zu Doe."

He flailed his arms and send a few kicks out, barely being able to get his feet off the ground, all while making some sound that I think, in his mind, was something Bruce Lee would do.

It was pathetic.

I couldn't help but laugh. Poor guy thought he was making people laugh with him. In reality, we were laughing at him, and how pathetic his stories would sound.

"So, you and your friends didn't like this,.." The Reporter paused for a second, "Reen character. I think I can understand that. You had mentioned before that his stories were somewhat unbelievable. I definitely see what you're saying. That last bit was completely farfetched." The Reporter told Jane while looking through his notes.

"So, when did you realize that something was going on? That you and your friends were not alone out there?" Jane repositioned herself on the hospital bed, grabbing her right leg in pain. "It was shortly after Reens little rant. I would say only an hour had passed by." Jane said to the reporter while repositioning herself, trying to get comfortable again. It was obvious to Jane that The Reporter was eagerly awaiting Jane to continue with her recanting. Maybe too interested?

Jane studied The Reporter for a moment. What was it about him that gave her such an unsettling feeling in the pit of her stomach? She found herself coming back to this same feeling many times throughout the interview. Each instance pushed aside, convincing herself it was nothing. 'It's just everything that happened. My brain automatically labels everyone as a threat.' She thought to herself over and over. The first time she had met him, her mind went into a frenzy. Almost like it had been trying to recall a distant memory that was buried just a bit too deep. And just like the unsettling feelings, she gives a quick dismissal, and she's back to telling her story.

We had just finished a bowl of weed when Luke left us to go use the trees as a bathroom. "Wow, I gotta hand it to you, Reen,"

Mike clapped as he continued, "you didn't go with him! Good for you, bud! We've finally settled it. The two of you don't help each other hold it while peeing." Reen laughed sarcastically and checked his watch. "It's ok," Rachel told him, "he's a big boy, I'm sure he's ok. He'll be back, probably ended up having to take a crap is all."

Luke had been gone for 20 minutes already, and Reen was getting worried. He started pacing back and forth. It was painstakingly clear that Reen was getting worried. "Knock it off dude." Jake demanded of Reen. "Your making me nervous now, and we're here, trying to have a good time." Reen turned, replying to Jake, "dude twenty minutes. He's been gone twenty minutes now, so I'm sorry if me being worried is upsetting your little shindig here, but it's been too long for a quick piss." Jake promised Reen that if Luke wasn't back in another fifteen minutes, then we would all go look for him.

Reen agreed and sat down in front of the fire pit with a fresh beer. But fifteen minutes had come and passed, and Luke had not returned. Then another ten minutes, and still no Luke. That's when Jake realized they needed to go looking for him. So myself, Jake, Mike and Reen set out to go find him.

"Luke!" Reen shouted through the woods. "Dude, let's go man! Where are you?" Jake looked around shouting, "Dude this ain't cool, knock it the fuck off already, its not funny, and I know funny." They searched around every tree, every stone, and every bush. Until they came up to a tree that had an arrow stuck in it. There were a few slash marks on its bark. And it didn't take them long to find Luke, either.

Reen spun around and called Luke's name again when he suddenly stopped. "What the-" he wipes his forehead with his hand as he feels something wet drip onto his head. "What the hell is this? Mike, dude,.. flashlight" Mike shines the flashlight in Reens direction replying "yeah what's up?" Wiping his forehead with his other hand, he yells to Mike, "bring it over here, let me see it."

Mike reaches Reen to see him staring at his hands. He shines the light onto Reen's hands. "Is that-" Jake interrupted Mike before he could finish. "Yo, what's that up there?" Mike shines the light into the treetops. After a few side to side movements of the flashlight, Mike stops. The light removes enough darkness to reveal a body hanging upside down.

Blood slowly dripped onto Reen's forehead. Shocked, Reen dashes backwards and trips over Luke's head. The eyes were wide open, blank and lifeless. The pupils dilated. I don't actually remember seeing any color to them. Just the deepness in the black of his eyes. The first time you see that, the emptiness of a dead person's eyes, it seems like it's never ending.

His teeth pressed firmly against each other, as if he had been biting down through an extremely painful ordeal. The cut at the base of his neck was jagged and rough. It was clear to Mike they did this in a slow process. His head, soaked in its own blood, laid in a pool of it.

Mike and Jake shined the flashlight into the tree at Luke's body. His ankles tied it to the branch, his arms fell limp, dangling towards the ground. His hands were missing, as well as his shirt. There was a large symbol carved into his chest.

I don't think I need to tell you just how clear it was that this was no accident. People don't tie themselves to a tree and mutilate themselves. Then I remembered the stories. I remembered the warnings. My mother's voice was ringing through my head. 'Bad people live down that road.' And I,... we, were now deep down that road.

"Wait a minute, what's that on his chest?" I asked. "I don't know," Jake replied. His eyes fixated on Luke's lifeless, hanging corpse. "Everyone step back." I instructed. Looking down as I backed up, Mike's light went on to the ground. We realized quickly that the stories may have, in fact, been true. My heart pounded. Each beat felt as though it was about to burst clear out of my chest. My stomach churned when I noticed what was under Luke's body. There was a giant pentagram. Luke's head lay in the middle, his blood seeping into the dirt. I turned to the bush next to me and threw up. My head spinning, thoughts racing. Luke was dead and as I threw up, all I could think of was that poor girl 20 years ago.

We all were next.....

Chapter 8

Reen's yelling was heard clearly as I spit the last little bits of vomit out of my mouth. "Fuck! Fuck! Luke is gone. What the fuck is happening? Is this one of your fucking jokes, Jake? This is sick! Real fucking sick" His eyes were filling with rage as he stared at Jake waiting for an answer. "Dude, this is beyond me. My jokes are harmless, besides Luke came out here on his own." Jake replied as he shined his lights through the dark woods. "Someone else is out here, maybe more, and they couldn't have gotten far yet." Jake didn't sound like he was sure of what he had just said, and neither was I. "How can you be sure they didn't get too far? We don't know when this happened, and how can we be sure it wasn't just one person?" Mike asked with a shaking voice. Reen took the flashlight from Mike's hand as he moved closer to the blood, trying not to step in it.

"No, Jake's right," I said. I took the flashlight from Reen and shined it at Luke's body. "This had to have just happened. The blood is still draining. There's only so much in the body." I went over to Luke's head and put my hand on his forehead. "He's still warm to the touch. Couldn't have been too long. We need to call the police before anything else happens."

"Not yet, we don't." Reen said. He took the flashlight back as he looked around. He shined the light between the trees as he continued, "If this guy's still close, we need to find him.

Now." Reen's response was typical of him. Constantly trying to take care of problems himself. But this was more than some kid at school, or a customer at his work. This was murder, and we needed help. Actual help.

"There's no way this was one person," Jake said sternly at Reen. "Luke is,... was a big guy. I'm pretty sure he could have fought off one guy. And look how high he is. That takes help. This took at least two, maybe three people. We're pretty close to everyone else. So why didn't we hear him yell for help?" Jake was right. Luke was a big guy, so one person couldn't have gotten him up there. His body was a good thirty feet above the ground. I tried looking for footprints around the blood to see if we could figure out how many people there were. None. Not one foot print.

It made no sense. How could they not leave a bloody trail? "Where are the footprints?" I asked. "How can there be no footprints?"

"So you didn't call the police?" The Reporter asks Jane. "No," she responded. "I preferred to. Right then and there, but with all the confusion, we settled on trying to figure out where the people that did this to Luke had gone. That and all our phones were at the party." The reporter looks up from his notes as a nurse walks into the room.

"Well, good afternoon Jane. And how are we feeling today?" Jane sighs and grabs her leg. Her eyes and face filled with the look of stress. "Awe, you poor thing, is it feeling weird, or just painful?" The nurse asks while moving closer to the IV bag next to the bed, checking the level of saline. Jane searches for the right words. The pain is there, of course, but not where it should be. The words Jane needs seem almost out of reach, unreal; nonexistent. Her eyes lift to the nurse. "A bit of both, I guess," she explains, "but definitely painful. You wouldn't expect to feel the pain without, well, anything there I guess you could say." She grabs her leg as she pulls herself to a seated position on the bed.

"I'm going to go grab a coffee for a minute. We can continue more a little later, Jane." The Reporter nods at the nurse as he leaves the room, putting on his old baseball cap, and leaving his computer by his chair. "Am I supposed to feel my leg still?" Jane clenches onto what's left of her leg as a sharp pain seems to run the length of where the rest used to be. The knee remains, but not too much after that.

"It's completely normal to still feel the body part after it's removed. Your brain still has to get used to the fact that your leg is missing, Jane." The nurse explains as she finishes changing the IV bag. "We'll get you some medicine and the doctor should be in shortly to look at your leg. After that, I'll change the dressing. Are you hungry yet?" Jane hesitates for a moment. Food? Could she really be hungry? Her stomach growled, loud enough for the nurse to take notice. Yes, she is hungry, but she doesn't actually want to eat. Jane looks through the opening in the blinds. Surprisingly, there's a comforting feeling she gets now from the sight of the sun. There may be comfort building, but not enough to find the strength to eat. She looks back at the nurse, lifts her eyes and answers with a bit of uncertainty, "no, not really."

The nurse puts her hands on her hips, "now Janey, you have to eat something. You've been here for three days and have not touched anything but water." She moves closer to Jane, placing her hand onto the bed rails. Using a calm and comforting voice, she speaks to Jane as a nurturing mother, "I know you've been through a lot dear, and your thinking about all those friends you've been telling the reporter about, but right now, you must do what's best for you. You need to eat something." Jane turns her head to the window, staring out at the sky once again, "I'm sure I'll eat sometime. I just feel so nauseous still. Every time I close my eyes, all I can see is blood and those headlights. It really kills the appetite."

A knock at the door gets Jane's attention. She looks to see the sheriff at the door. "I just wanted to come and check on you today, see how you're holding up." He tells Jane as he walks into the room.

He removes his hat walking up to the side of her bed. "Hi Uncle Steve, I'm doing ok, I guess. I'm just trying to cope. Any word on Jake? Did you find him yet?" He leans down and kisses her forehead. "Not yet, sweetie, but I'm looking." Steve has been a close friend of the family since Jane was in the second grade. Since her parents had no siblings, Steve was the closest Jane could get to an 'Uncle'. "We got every available man out there," he continued. "If he's out there, we'll find him."

His words are meant to be reassuring, but Jane finds them less than comforting. She knows it's been three days since she last saw Jake, and she knows his time is running out. "You just get your rest," her uncle tells her, "you need it".

He leans down and kisses her forehead before leaving her room, just barely missing bumping into The Reporter. Steve stops suddenly, turning back, looking at the reporter, trying to get a better look at him. He places his hat back onto his head as he slowly walks down the hospital hallway, sure that he knows the man from somewhere. He just can't seem to place it.

A gentle hand on his shoulder grasps his attention, pulling him back into reality. A few friendly greetings are exchanged between the sheriff and a doctor dressed in casual attire. The unsettling feeling of remembrance now fades into a vague memory, and all thoughts of the man now vanish.

"How is she?" the reporter asks Jane's nurse. "She's doing better," she answers, "but she needs to eat something, and soon." As Jane's nurse leaves the room, she turns to Jane and says, "The medicine should start to take effect shortly, and Dr. Anders will be in to see you with in the hour. After that, you will need to eat. The infection is harder to fight off if you're not eating. I'll bring you something light, but you must eat it." As she leaves the room, she leans towards the reporter. Placing a hand on his shoulder, she whispers, "maybe you can help her get her appetite back."

He takes a seat beside the far end of the bed and gets settled in. "Jane, I know this must be difficult for you. I can't imagine what you're going through. We do not have to keep going with this interview if you don't want to." He pauses for a moment, debating the next thing he's about to say. He knows he should help the nurse, he knows what's right, but for him, it's the story. He tells himself to keep her comfortable. He needs this story, so he takes a deep breath and finishes. "I'm not going to tell you to eat or make you feel uncomfortable, so just let me know when you want to stop." She turns her head away from the window and looks at the reporter. She sighs, lifting herself up, she tells him "no, this needs to be done. Other people need to know it's not just some story your parents tell you about. What happened that night was terrible, and if I don't tell people what happened, it will just keep repeating. Jake would want people to know what happened to him." She leans back on her pillows, trying to get comfortable. "Then we can continue when ever your ready." He places his laptop on his legs, opening it. "Lets see," he says as he searches through his notes. "Where were we?"

Reading through his notes, he asks her why she didn't call the police. "Like I said before, our phones were back at the cemetery. That and Reen was determined to find out how many there were." He raises his eyes from the screen. "And where you able to tell?" She looks out the window once more. "No, somehow they left no tracks. All that was left was an arrow in the tree and Luke."

After searching the entire area surrounding the tree, I had decided it was time to get back to the others. I wasn't going to take no for an answer, either. "Reen, I know you're upset," I said, placing my hand on his shoulder. "But it's time to get back. We need to call the police and let them handle this." He looked at me angrily. "Fine," his reply was reluctant, but he knew I was right.

So we headed back to the cemetery. Mike seemed to be relieved to get out of those woods. The first thing he did was run up to Rachel. "Where's Luke?" she asked. "Did you find him?" He grabbed onto her shoulder and pulled her close to him. "It's time to go, like now. Right now," he told her in a whisper. "Luke's dead," Rachel jumped back, staring into Mike's eyes. She could tell he was serious, and Mike wasn't someone to joke around, especially like this.

"What!" she yelled. "How?"

I went straight for my phone. I kept pushing that stupid power button, but it wouldn't turn on. The damn thing was dead. Dan and Josh were trying to figure out what was going on. I guess in all the excitement, no one mentioned anything to them. "YO!" Josh screamed. "Does anyone want to tell me what the fuck is going on?" You could hear the confusion turning into anger in his voice. "You guys disappear into the woods looking for Luke, and now you're out here with no Luke, acting like someone just died." I immediately stopped and looked at him. He could tell right away what he said was the truth. "Oh my god,... the fuck happened?" He started searching the trees while he asked me.

Reen came over to us, fidgeting with his phone. His anger had finally subsided, now there was just fear in his eyes. They were wide as he said, "who's got a phone? Mine's dead." Dan was patting around his pockets, looking for his phone, when the screaming started. I remember all he could say was "were the hell is my-" I had looked up just in time to see an arrow penetrate through his left eye. Everything went into a slow motion. I watched in horror as Dan went limp, slowly falling backwards. I'm pretty sure he was dead before he hit the ground. Rachel was in the back screaming, and once again I was face to face with a lifeless body. I wiped the blood off my face and looked down to see Dan's body twitch.

We had little time to think or take in what had just happened. Time finally seemed to catch back up with my mind, and within seconds, we were being bombarded by arrows. They came from all directions, hitting Reen twice, one in each of his arms. Nothing too serious. I don't think they were trying to kill us then. With the arrow in Dan's eye, I was certain that they had good aim. I think they were trying to separate us. Get us to scatter, to not think about where we were. Where we were going.

And it worked.

We ran around hectically, trying to find each other. Every time we would seem to get close, more arrows would separate us. "Get home. I'll meet you there." Jake yelled at me from across the field. He tried to stay close to me, but there was too much confusion, too much chaos. I knew Josh's car was down the street a bit, so I was okay with being with Josh. Rachel and Mike had gotten separated as well. She was with Josh and me, while Mike was with Jake and Reen. We ran for the tree line as fast as we could. Once we were there, I watched as Reen was shot again with an arrow, this time in his leg. I'll never know how they all made it to Mike's car, but that was the last time I ever saw Reen.

Well, that was the last time I saw him; alive.

Chapter 9

Once we entered the woods, we stopped to see what was happening with Chris and Worm. I was hoping they had made it back to their car. I searched for any sign of them. Then I saw them stepping out from within the woods.

They were displayed in large, darkened jackets. A heavy hood covered their faces. A bow hung around each of their shoulders. I noticed immediately that they were all converging toward the center of the field. That's when I noticed Chris and Worm.

Both lay face down on the ground, each with a single arrow embedded in their back, just above the tailbone. One of the hooded figures pulled out a large machete, while another one pulled out a rope. "Please be dead already, please be dead," I whispered, trying not to be heard. "They were never that lucky, Jane. What the hell is going on?" Rachel asked me. I could hear the uneasiness in her voice.

"Please be dead," I repeated.

The one with the rope leaned over Worm and turned him around onto his back. Worm shrieked as the arrow pierced through his body, surfacing through the flesh of his abdomen. With the rope now wrapped around Worm's neck, I heard the one with the machete yell out, "lift him to his feet." His voice was deep and demanding. Josh covered Rachel's mouth, knowing she was about to scream. I looked back and saw them lift Chris to his feet as well, making him watch Worm's unavoidable death.

They leaned Worm onto one figure's back, keeping him in place with the rope, now tight around his neck. I watched as the machete sliced down Worm's shirt. Blood spilled out, staining the shirt as they pulled it off him. Worm screamed as an abrupt, powerful swing from the machete sliced across his stomach. His intestines fell to the ground as his body convulsed.

"You sick mother fuckers!" Chris yelled. "Sick are we?" the man with the machete reacted, turning to Chris. He stepped close to Chris and clutched his neck. "I'll teach you sick boy," he told him in a coarse and violent voice. He stepped closer, now towering over Chris as he wiped the machete clean across Chris's face. He turned to Worm's lifeless body and swung the machete into his chest. With two hands he pulled downward, making a clean slice down Worm's chest. I could feel my stomach turning as I heard Rachel's screams under Josh's arm. The man tossed his machete down and reached for Worm's chest. I could hear the ribs cracking as he opened his chest. He stepped out of the way and the figure holding Chris up pushed his face into Worm's body. Then they covered him with Worm's intestines, lifting him back to his feet. Finally, they shoved what they could fit into his mouth. "Hows that for sick?" the man asked as he pulled the arrow out of Chris's back.

"Lay him on his back and make his eyes stay open!" the man ordered. One figure, this one much smaller, pulled out a small hunting knife and knelt down over Chris's head. His knees squeezed against the sides of his head. "Don't move, else you go blind," he yelled and then proceeded to remove both eyelids. The four of them stood over him, pulling out small axes and hacked away at Chris, limb by limb.

"Enough! It's time to find the rest of them. They didn't get too far. Find them, make them pay for their trespassing." The man ordered. "And what of these two?" The smallest of the four asked in what sounded almost like a child's voice. "Take what you will, but leave this one's head. I want his skull. Bring theirs hearts for Mother. She'll be pleased with this one's." Hovering over Chris's lifeless body, he stared down at it, almost chuckling, "He had quite a bit of fight left in him." He ordered.

"Always thinking of Mother, aren't you? Ever since they left, you've been sucking up to her." The man with the rope said. I could hear the sarcasm and hate in his voice. "Watch your tone with me, Jeff. Out here you abide by me. That's the way it is, was, and always will be." I knew right there that the stories were true, and I was beginning to understand the system they used. "You're just a brother to me, Mark. Just a snot nose spoiled brat." Jeff yelled as he stood up, taking a bite out of Worm's arm. I couldn't hold it in anymore. The bite made me throw up. "At home, I'm your brother, yes, but out here, I rule. This is my time. I am your leader, your guide, your god. You will do as I say and nothing else. Now, seal your mouth or I'll seal it for you. Do I make myself clear, little boy?" Mark demanded a respectful response, but Jeff would have no part of it.

Although I was intrigued, I felt someone tugging on my arm, trying to get me to leave. Strangely, I was unable to take my eyes off them. Their presence was overwhelming, demanding of an audience. I watched as they scurried back and forth across the field, and I now had a name for two of them: Mark, the leader, and Jeff, the angry brother. But who were the others? I thought that the smallest might be a child. Maybe this was his first time actually killing people. It was a shame that they should bring a child into this life.

The other one didn't speak, just took orders and was gathering body parts while Mark and Jeff argued. What are they doing with the body parts? I thought, what did he mean by take what you will, and Mother will be pleased with this one's? I didn't get to think too long on those thoughts. My attention was quickly drawn back to the figures, as Jeff removed his hood.

He was bald and disfigured; badly. He had almost pointed ears, and his skin looked like it was burned, or scared. It was hard to tell from my distance, though it started coming more into focus as they came closer. They were getting much closer, but I still couldn't move. "Oh yeah, you've made yourself real clear," Jeff bickered. "You've got an attitude problem. You need to be adjusted. And I take orders from no man, not even from a god." Jeff got right up to Mark's face. It looked as if he was pressing his forehead against Marks. "Your protected by family law. That's the only reason you still breathe. Now do I make myself clear?" Jeff asked sternly as he stepped forward toward Mark. For a moment, I thought Mark would fall backwards, and Jeff would step right over him. Somehow, Mark stood his ground and kept his balance.

I could tell right there that I was wrong. I believed Mark to be the largest, but clearly Jeff towered over him. That's when verbal arguments became heated physical violence between the two brothers. Mark's head leaned back and quickly swung forward, smacking into Jeff's jaw. I could hear the cracking sound from my position in the woods, so I know that blow should have hurt. But it barely fazed Jeff. He took a few steps back, then lunged at Mark. The two of them were now in a brutal battle.

That's when I was pulled backwards.

Josh had grabbed my arm and took off running. It knocked me on my back as he pulled me along. The fighting siblings disappeared in the dark as I got farther and farther. "Stop! Let me up!" I instructed. A moment later, we stopped. I got to my feet and was able to see the need to leave on Josh's face. Rachel was spinning in circles, one hand on her hip, the other on her forehead. She was as pale as a ghost. "Oh, my god. They killed them. They're all dead! Who were those people? Why are they doing this to us?" She kept repeating herself over and over as she paced in circles.

"I thought the stories were just stories. That, that just made it very real. We need to find Jake and Mike." I rambled on. "They need our help. Reen is with them and he's hurt. We have to find them." I said to Josh as I grabbed Rachel and hugged her, trying to calm her down. She burst into tears as her knees gave out. I knelt down in front of her, placed my hands on the sides of her head. "I had no idea it was true, Rach," I told her in a soft, apologetic voice. "Rach, I swear, I didn't know."

"We need to get the hell out of here right now!" Josh told me. His voice was shaken, his nerves had been shot. "Jake said go home, he'll be fine, probably already heading to your house. Now come on Jane, did you actually see any of what just happened? You were watching, weren't you?" He paced back and forth as he tried to urge Rachel back to her feet. "Yes, I saw." My response was quiet, but angry. Josh had an attitude, and now I did too. I started to use my hands to talk as I continued. "Made me sick is what it did, and two of my friends are now dead. Another is freaking out, so give me just a second. Where's your car?" I pulled Rachel to her feet and pushed her hair behind her ears. "Josh is right, Rach. We have to go. They're going to kill us. Can you keep up with us now? Please?" I asked, as I wiped the tears from her eyes. "He was eating him, he was fucking eating his arm. What the hell is wrong with those people?" Rachel was trying to gather herself together, but in those words, I knew she was still back there. Stuck in her own terror.

"Hey Rach, you like your arms, don't you? Want to keep them, don't you? Or would you rather let Mister Wrinkly Face back there gnaw on them? No? Yeah, I didn't think so. And know what? Neither do I. So, enough is enough. Okay? You can freak out all you want in my car, but now is the time to go. I don't want to die in these back woods cause you can't pull yourself together. Let's go, now!" Josh made his point sternly as he grabbed her arm and pulled her along. We scampered through the woods, trying not to make too much noise. Which turns out, is very hard to do when you're in the woods during the middle of the night.

Maybe it was the racing heartbeat, but I swear, I could hear every breaking branch, every dead, dried up leaf. Seemed as though we stepped on every single one of them.

"That was rude, wasn't it?" I whispered to Josh as I caught up to him. "Look," I explained, "I know you're scared, but so is she, and so am I Josh." I held onto Rachel's hand as we came close to where we had parked. I started recognizing where I was, but something was wrong, something was noticeably off.

We reached the road and Josh stopped dead in his tracks. It took a second for us to realize what was wrong. "Where's his car?" Rachel asked nervously. "Did we go the wrong way, Jane?" I looked around, hoping we just over shot the car, but it was nowhere in sight. "Shit! Shit, shit, shit! Where the hell is my car? This is where we parked, isn't it?" I knew what he was thinking. Hell, I was thinking the same thing.

They were not letting us leave. We were all going to die in that field.

Chapter 10

"Wow, that's pretty scary." The Reporter says. "Disgustingly detailed, but horrifying, truly, horrifying." Jane nodded, her eyebrows lifted slightly. "I could cut back on the details, if you want." she said. "I don't know how detailed you want your story to be, so I'm trying not to leave anything out." Jane searches the bed for the nurse's call box as she continues, "So, is this is a book you're writing? How come you don't want to tell the story on the news?"

He closes the laptop and glances out the window. "It's been a long day, Jane, and you need your rest. Why don't we call it a day and pick up again tomorrow?" He turns his focus to Jane with a small smile on his face. She knows he's hiding something. It's easy for her to tell; she just can't figure out what it is.

"He's right Janey, you do need your rest." The nurse said as she entered the room. "I see you've called for a nurse. Is everything alright dear?" She leans over and presses a button next to the bed. "I'm in a lot of pain, nurse. Am I able to get more medicine yet?" Jane asks with discomfort in her voice. "Please Jane, call me Paulette. How about I get you something for the pain, and you eat something? Can you do that for me?" She places a hand on the edge of the bed as Jane sighs.

"Yes, I can do that Paulette. I am a little hungry now." Her attention is quickly diverted to the sirens outside the hospital.

The Reporter stands up to the window to try to see what's going on. "Oh my, he doesn't look good at all." He said. "It amazes me how cruel people can be to each other." The Reporter continued as he closes the case for the laptop. He pulls his jacket on and turns to Nurse Paulette, "at least she's willing to eat something finally." She smiles. "What ever you said must have helped out somehow, Mr. Charles." He turns to Jane as he pulls the laptop over his shoulders, "you get some sleep Jane, I'll be back tomorrow, what time would be good for you?" She looks at the clock on the wall for a moment, "to be honest, anytime is fine. I won't be getting much sleep tonight. Every time I close my eyes, all I can see are those horrible people."

He places his baseball cap on his head and heads for the door. Turning to Jane, he reassures her, "don't worry Jane, you're safe here. They've got an officer right outside your door at all times. I guess it pays to have the sheriff as an uncle now, doesn't it?" Jane leans up in her bed and tells Charles - the reporter, "well, really, he's just a close friend of the family. See, I don't have any aunts or uncles. In fact, I've never met any of my other family members. My father always told me they had moved here from across the country before I was born. Him and Mom wanted a fresh start, away from the rest of the family. My understanding is that they didn't get along very well."

A knock at the door ends their conversation. "Hello, I brought you some food. Nurse Paulette said to make sure it was light. I understand that you're not feeling too good and might not be too hungry, so I brought you a little spaghetti and some jello. We've got some fruit punch for a drink, everybody loves the hospital's fruit punch! Oh, and can't forget the hot tea. That always makes me feel better. There's a little cream and sugar, and some honey and lemon if you prefer. Just let us know if there is anything else you need, okay hun?" She moves the tray close to Jane alongside the bed and heads for the door. "I'll be back in about an hour for the plates. Try to eat all your food now."

For the first time since her arrival, Jane finds herself alone. No nurse, no reporter, no friends. She grabs the television remote and flips through the channels. News, news, news. Never anything good on anymore, she tells herself. "Oh, we get the History channel." She speaks aloud. Not sure why she's talking to herself, she realizes Jake would be content right now. When the commercial ends, there is an autopsy show on. "At least something good is on." She says. She grabs the food tray and pulls it over her legs. Removing the lid, she knows she'll have to force the food down. Happy there's no meat, she wonders why she started talking to herself. Maybe because I've gotten used to someone being here, she thinks to herself. She picks up the fork and tries to eat some food, but all she can do is stare at it. "Poor Jake is probably so hungry right now." The thought of her friends makes it harder for her to eat, but she knows she must.

Fork full by fork full she forces it down.

"Oh, Jane!" a saddened voice calls from the doorway. She recognizes the voice as a smile comes across her face. "Mom!" she exclaims. "My poor baby girl. What did they do to you?" Jane's mom hurries over to her, leaning down to kiss her forehead. She places one hand on the bed rail and her other on Jane's leg, but her hand feels the bed instead. "Janey! Your leg!" Her hand covers her mouth as tears run down her face. "It's gone Mom. That's the only reason I'm still alive. Can we not talk about right now?" She hugs her mother tightly and tries to calm her down. "Your still alive and that's what matters, isn't it? I don't know why you even went back there. Didn't your father and I give you enough warnings?" She asked Jane.

"That doesn't matter, honey," her father says as he enters the room. "She's okay. I'm sure she's learned to stay far away from that place." He slowly limps over to Jane's bed. "Hi Daddy!" Jane says as her face begins to glow. She's happy to see her parents, but most of all, she's happy to know her father was up and moving around again. "I see you're feeling better, hows your knee, daddy?" He lifts his leg up and barely bends it a few times. "Feels brand new," he lies, "but don't worry about your ol' man. We're here for you, sweetheart."

Jane's mother turns to her husband and hugs him, whispering in his ear, "she's lost her leg, from the knee down." The disappointment and anger on his face is clear. "Don't you worry about a thing Jane, the docs will fix you up real good. Plenty of people still live active, significant lives, with only one leg.

You've always been the girl who doesn't give up. I know this won't slow you down at all." He leans down and kisses her forehead. "Besides, the things they do with prosthetic nowadays, you'll be up and moving around in no time."

"Did they find Jake? I need to know if they found him yet." Her eyes filled with tears as she asks her father. "We're not sure what's going on right now. Uncle Steve came and talked with us just a short time ago, Janey. They've been out all day looking for your friends." Her mother assures her that as soon as Jake is found, they will let her know.

Her father's teeth grinding catches her attention. "You need to stop grinding your teeth, Daddy, that's how they break." She tells him, as she has so many times before. He started grinding his teeth when Jane first moved out of the family house. She always figured it was because of nervousness. He had always been a protective father, and with Jane no longer living at home, she felt his nerves were clearly agitated. But it's been a few years since she moved out, and her father has not stopped grinding his teeth. The truth is, it had nothing to do with being nervous. His grinding of teeth is a side effect of Parkinson's disease. He knows this, but neither him, nor his wife have told Jane about his diagnosis.

"We have some visitors I see! I'm nurse Paulette, but you can call me Paully. And who are these fine people, Jane?" Sitting up, she introduces her parents to Nurse Paulette, starting with her mother.

"Well, you two have raised one fine lady here! Oh, and I see you have finally eaten something! How are you feeling?" Paulette walks over and puts on a pair of gloves; and then prepares a needle of medicine for Jane. "I feel better now that I got some food in my stomach." She replies. "Well, that's good to hear, Jane. My apologies on the wait for pain medicine, but there was an emergency down stairs that your doctor had to help with." She gives Jane a shot of morphine and turns to the trash can. "It seems they found a guy half beaten to death in a car, locked in the trunk. No driver, but at least they had the decency to leave the car at the hospital. Poor guy was cut up real bad. No telling how long he had been in that trunk." Nurse Paulette tells her parents as she discards the needle.

Jane's parents pay close attention as the nurse takes vital signs from Jane. "How's she doing Mrs. Paully?" Her mother asks. "For someone who just went through what your daughter has gone through, surprisingly well, and is keen to co-operate." She responds. "Most people shut down after such an ordeal, but not our Jane. Nope, she's even telling her story to that reporter; Mr. Charles." Nurse Paulette turns her attention back to Jane, "Well Jane, you know what to do if you need anything. Now, try to get yourself some rest, sweetheart." Paulette heads to the door and tells Jane's parents that visiting hours are ending and Jane needs some rest. "She hasn't been sleeping much these past few days, and the medicine I gave her should help her sleep. Should be kicking in now." Her parents agree and say goodnight to Jane. Before her parents can leave, Jane falls asleep.

It's the first time she's been able to sleep so deeply. She was only awakened twice throughout the night by nightmares. Before she knows it, it's morning. She leans up in her bed and turns toward the door. Her foot now placed her foot on the floor. She slides herself to the edge of the bed. Looking around, she finds a pair of crutches leaning against a chair by her bed. She pauses for a moment to think. "What are you doing, Jane?" She says to herself. "Screw it. Got to start sometime, right?" She leans forward, grabbing the crutches propping them under her arm. She can feel her leg begin to wobble as she stands up, leaning her weight against the crutches. Her other leg trembles, shaking almost uncontrollably as she takes each step toward the bathroom. The excitement overwhelms her as she reaches the bathroom.

The presence of the doctor startled Jane as she walks out of the bathroom to see him and Charles sitting in the room. "Feeling adventurous today, are we?" Charles tells her with excitement in his voice. "It's good to see you're moving around now, Jane. So tell me, how's that leg feeling today?" The doctor asks her while opening her medical chart. "Pretty weird," she says, "just hurts where there's nothing actually there. Know what? I will say this, though. It's weird, you know, walking around on crutches without both feet." He nods and replaces her chart. "Its something to get used to," he says, "always takes a bit. We can try a prosthetic leg a little later, if you want. The timing may be a little early, but we can at least see how it feels around the muscle. Why don't you come over and sit down so I can look at that wound?"

He removes the bandages, trying not to cause her any unnecessary pain. His movements are slow as he examines the stitches. Curiosity kicks in as Jane leans forward and watches with wide eyes.

"How's it look, doc? Think I could be getting out of here soon?" He gently places her leg back on the bed and smiles. "You're healing quite well. Might get out of here soon enough. I hear your parents gave you a visit yesterday." Filled with joy, she tells him, "yes they did! Finally got back from their vacation. Bet they never take another one now." She laughs as she realizes she still has a sense of humor. "Well, I know I would have a hard time." The doctor tells her. "Looks like I can go ahead and get out of here. I think you just need another day, two tops, but we'll try to get you out of here tomorrow if you'd like." Jane nods and smiles as the doctor leaves the room.

"Well, that's some good news, isn't it?" Charles says. "Very much so!" she replies. Charles pulls out his laptop and sits down as he opens it.

"Okay, were where we?"

Chapter 11

Josh was already nervous, and now his frustration was easily felt by all of us. All he wanted to do was go home. That's all any of us wanted to do. So I don't blame him for the way he was acting. Every turn we made, he would get more and more anxious. I guess that's normal when you're lost. Our first mistake, crossing that road, and I tried to tell him, but he didn't want to hear anything I had to say. The second mistake, staying quiet and following him blindly.

"Josh, you have us going in circles. You need to slow down. We can't keep up with you." Rachel pleaded for him to take a break. "I'm not waiting around for those freaks to come back for us. If you want to die out here, you have fun, but I'll keep moving." His response was bitter and struck a nerve with Rachel. She squeezed my hand and whispered to me, "say something Jane, please."

She was a wreck, and he wasn't making any of this easier. I gave Rachel a gentle squeeze on her shoulder and gestured for her to take a break from walking. My anger finally at its tipping point I caught up to Josh. "That's a fucked up thing to say Josh. There are two other people here. We need to work together to get out of here. Do you even know where you're going?" I snapped as I grabbed his arm, spinning him around. "Look at us! Look around you. We are lost, and you're making things worse." My voice at it's loudest, but I didn't care. I was pissed, and I kept going. "We should have never crossed that road. Could be out of here by now." For the first time since we all split up, Josh was finally listening to someone other than himself. Maybe I shouldn't have yelled at him. Basically placing all blame on him. Or maybe it was exactly what we needed at that moment.

He looked around in a circle, convinced he was heading the right way. His face filled with anger once more, as he realized he had no idea where we were. "We go that way," he pointed behind himself. "The way we were going, the main road is that way, I'm sure of it." He turned back and continued on his way. "No Josh," I insisted. "It's not. We've been walking this way, and that way for twenty minutes now." Pointing towards the road, I wanted my next point to be understood clearly. "We've crossed that fucking road four times, and I'm tired. Rachel is tired and not to mention falling apart over here." I continued yelling through the woods, not caring who heard me. At that point, I just wanted to stop and think. Retrace our steps. Get home.

I sat Rachel down on a fallen tree and knelt down in front of her. "Look at you Rach," I said in a soft voice. "Your make-up is running down!" I used my thumb to wipe the tears from her eyes. "Don't worry, we'll be alright. Just a little farther and we'll be home free." It was obvious she didn't believe me, not a single word. Hell, I didn't believe me either.

I rubbed her arms trying to calm her down. She was shaking vigorously. I brushed her hair behind her ears and placed my hands on her cheeks. Her teeth were chattering enough to feel the vibration running through my hands. "I need you to try and focus now, okay? Josh is right we need to keep moving or we'll die in these woods." She raised her eyes to me as tears filled them. "Which way Jane?" She asked. "We've been going in circles for so long, I,... I don't know where we are anymore." I stood her to her feet holding her hands and told her, "we need to go back the way we came, and follow the road," she interrupted me "The road? Jane are you nuts, won't they see us on the road?" I looked back at Josh and could see the frustration in his eyes. "We follow the road, staying close to the woods. Out of sight. Either way we need to go back." I was barely able to finish speaking before Josh lost his cool. He pushed his way between us shouting as loud as he could.

"Go back the way we came! You've lost it Jane. All I keep hearing from you is go back, go back! Shouldn't have crossed the road! Fine you want to go back, then let's do it your way!" He grabbed my arm and pulled me along. "Let's go this way, let's go this way," he mumbled as I pulled my arm back. I stopped as we neared the road. I don't think Josh even saw the head lights, but I did. "Josh-" I whispered. "No, you want the road? Here it is! Are you happy now?" He yelled as he turned around and stepped backwards into the road.

Each hair on my arm stood on end. My arms reached out, desperately trying to get him to calm down, even for a brief moment. Nothing was working. Josh would not stop. Each step backwards brought him closer to the center of the road. With each step I checked the headlights, and with each step the lights grew closer. I reached my arms out, watching in horror.

An old suv raced toward Josh, accelerating as it struck him. His body folded onto the hood, head smacking into the center. Blood shot out from his nose and mouth. His feet flew out from beneath the front bumper as he tumbled over the length of the vehicle. I tried not to scream, but couldn't hold it in. The vehicle slammed on its breaks drowning out our screams as Josh's body bounced around on the ground.

Rachel and I stepped back a few feet, hoping that it was just someone passing through that hit Josh. We found out that wasn't the case when the suv backed up and over Josh. His body twisted around, leaving his head facing us, his eyes open. Our eyes linked as I stared into his, wondering if he was still alive. A considerable lump formed in my throat as I watched him blink. It only grew worse with the realization of what was about to unfold.

Pure terror.

The headlights of the suv cleared away the darkness of the road as they stepped out from the vehicle. One of them went to the back as the other walked up to Josh. He knelt down and removed his hood. I recognized the mangled skin on his face. It was Jeff. "I think this one's already dead," he said, calling out to the other one. "Such a pity," he said as he reached for Josh's face. With a firm grasp of his chin, he lifts Josh's face. "He's gonna miss the fun!" Jeff turned around to the suv as a familiar voice responded to him. "Did you check? Or are you just assuming?" Mark asked sarcastically. "Where's the other rope? There's only one in here."

Fear came over me as I watched, remembering what they did to Chris and Worm. "We used it on that skinny one earlier. But we can make do with what we got right here!" Jeff yelled as he grabbed Josh's hair, pulling his head back and forth. "Ah, this one is still alive!" Jeff said with cheer in his voice as Josh blinked and moaned. "He can't move, but he's awake!" Mark walked up with rope and an axe in his hand.

"Cover your eyes, Rachel," I said, wishing I could look away. In truth, I knew looking away would have done no good. The sound of the axe cutting through bone and striking the asphalt churned my stomach. They started with his hands and feet, just above the ankles. Then they went for his arms. First at the elbow, then the shoulders. His legs went next, knees first, then the hip. It seemed they were trying to keep him alive as long as possible.

I watched in disbelief as Jeff stood above Josh's torso and pulled out a large knife. "This is the best part, boy! Let's see what goodies you've got inside!" Jeff laughed as he dug the knife into Josh's abdomen. Josh gargled as blood spurted from his mouth. "It's like a pinata boy!" The sound of Jeff's voice echoed through the trees as his laughter became more and more intense. "Hey Ma, you want liver tonight?" Mark yelled to the car. A faint voice of a female rung out from the suv, "Take all the goods inside, they'll make a wonderful stew for lunch." Her voice was coarse and old, sending frigid shivers down my spine.

The clinging of a last swing from the axe interrupted my fear. It struck the ground loudly as Josh's head rolled away from his body. Jeff quickly went to the back of the suv and returned with a railroad spike and large mallet. A few strikes from the mallet, and holes are poked through each of the severed limbs. He pulls a rope through each hole. Mark took the limbs to the back of the suv and tied them to the bumper. It reminded me of the cans people hang from cars when they get married. Around the front, Jeff used Josh's intestines to secure his head to the deer guard. Even though it was dark in those woods, I could still see how pale my skin became as they used Josh's blood to write the words:

Newly Separated across the back window.

Chapter 12

We laid as still as we could on that cold ground. The dead leaves surrounded our bodies as we tried not to make a sound. I could hear them arguing about what to do with Josh's remains, well what was left of him, anyway. Jeff was insisting on keeping it. He said they would make a great shelf for his collectibles, whatever that meant. Mark argued for his dogs. "Its good meat for the dogs," he claimed, "and the bones will keep them busy for hours." The old lady leaned her head out of the window, "toss it to the side, He'll send the animals to clean your mess." She demanded. "Always cleaning up after you two. What thanks have you sent? Shelves and lamps to decorate a room? Or treats for your precious little mutts? Too ignorant to see the more important matters at hand. Toss him out, and grab the two in them woods while you're at it." She snapped in a harsh voice, reassuring that she was in control of the two brothers. "You two will make up for your impotence with the scared little one."

I couldn't believe she knew we were there. We had laid so still, desperately trying not to make a sound. Maybe it was those damned dead leaves. Doesn't anyone clean them up? Mark turned towards us. I could feel his blank eyes searching for us. He stepped closer, the twigs cracking under the weight of his feet echoed over our heads. "What two?" Jeff asked. "This one was alone," Mark added, his eyes still combing the woods. We laid still, hoping they didn't see us. Maybe they'll think we left during their game of murder, I had hoped.

"Too busy playing dolls to notice the two girls hiding? And I thought I taught you better than that. Do you two have any idea what happens if they get away? What they'll bring back to our land? Then everyone will forget why they stay out. Such a pity, so close to the main road." I couldn't believe what she just said. So close to the main road? Maybe Josh was going the right way after all. I thought if I had not argued with him, we might just be out of this hellhole. He would still be alive, and we could be on our way home.

The two brothers made their way towards us. This was it, I thought, now or never. All I could think was we need to get out of here. So I grabbed Rachel's hand and stood up to run as fast as we could. I can still feel the impact of that kid's arm on my neck. I was so caught up in the moment that I had completely forgotten about him. He knocked the wind out of me and we hit the ground, hard. Rachel was gasping for air as he stood above us looking downward, still not uttering a single word. I lifted myself up on my elbows as I readied to kick our way free.

As I prepared to kick, I felt a large hand on my head, gripping a portion of my hair. I reached behind and felt a massive arm. The screams from Rachel and I were futile. No one was around to hear our pleas. Yet we still screamed as loud as we could. "Quite your mouth, child." Jeff's voice rang in my ears. I swung my arms from side to side, trying to connect with his knees. My father would tell me all men will fall when their knee gives way. Sadly, he never told me what to do when they expect it. He pulled me to my feet as Mark lifted Rachel to her knees. "Should we do this now?" His voice was deeper this time. Maybe because we were so close now. "No! Leave her alone!" I begged. He pulled a large dagger from his side and placed it against her neck. "Not here. She's been through enough for now. We'll bring them home, let her sleep before her friend's big moment". The old lady's voice was more gentle this time, coarse, but almost caring.

And then everything went black. They placed something over my head. My hands now tied behind my back. I felt a tightening around my neck. I struggled as he led me to the suv and threw me into the back. Feeling Rachel tossed in beside me was somewhat comforting. It let me know she was still alive, at least for now. I moved closer to her and whispered, "we'll get out of this, don't worry".

I knew I was lying to her, but I was trying to keep her calm. The suv turned wildly, tossing what felt like gardening tools towards us. That vehicle hit every bump in the road, and then it seemed to bear off the road. Running over falling trees and rocks, anything that stood in its way. It seemed like an eternity before we finally came to a stop. The back door opened, and I felt those large hands grab my ankles. The barking of dogs filled the air as they pulled me out of the suv feet first. For a brief second, I felt weightless, but that ended quickly as my head hit the ground. Rachel's legs landed on mine, waking me from my encounter with the rocky ground.

I must have been unconscious for a little while. I don't remember my legs being bound, nor the rope that now went around my chest and under my arms. As they dragged us inside, I heard Rachel screaming. The barking dogs were getting closer. The sound of their paws connecting against the ground came to a halt when I heard a slight whistle. Before I knew it, the dogs were right over me. I could feel their noses pressing into my body, like they were testing out a new chew toy before sinking their teeth in. "Not for you dog." Mark roared.

They pulled us up the front stairs step by step. Might have been more considerate if they picked us up at least, but I guess that's not an option when you're being dragged to your death. The door creaked as it opened and an old man said, "More quests?" We stopped moving as Jeff replied. "That's the last of them, dad." The old man walked away, struggling to take each step as his cane struck the floor. "Well, toss them in the cellar, suppers almost ready. And go clean that blood off your hands. I like a clean table."

The door opened, the sound that Rachel's body made when hitting each step pierced through my ears. It sounded like she was thrown. Now it was my turn. They lifted me to my feet, hands placed firmly on my back. I tensed up, knowing what was about to happen, when the old lady stepped into the house.

"Not that one. She stays with me." Not sure what she liked about me, but it seemed like she was trying to protect me. Out in the woods orders were snapped by Mark, but here, she had a firm grasp on what would and wouldn't happen. "Bring her to me," she ordered, "and get ready for supper. We're having meat stew tonight".

I felt a gentle hand on my shoulder, guiding me towards which way to move. She removed what looked like a cloth bag from my head, tossing it to the side. "Oh child," she said. "It's a joyful day in the home of the Beans. Now, you've heard the dogs, correct? And you've seen what my boys can do, so don't you fuss or run, and no harm shall come to you. Understand?" I nodded my head yes, but she wasn't having any of that. "Is that how your parents raised you? To not speak when a grandmother speaks to you?" I looked at her, unsure of how to respond. "Well, child?" She urged for a response. "I have no grandmother, no uncles, no aunts." I responded. "Oh shush now, yes you do. Everyone has a grandmother, and I have lots of grandchildren. You just don't know it yet."

She turned me around and began untying the rope across my chest. I thought about waiting for her to untie my hands and slamming my elbow into her face, but she was right. I knew those two would surely finish me before I could reach the driveway.

She reached down and untied the rope from my ankles. "Well now, look at you," she said. "All grown up, and mature. Ready to help grow the family, aren't you?" She sounded joyful, like she thought I was part of their sick family. I didn't respond. I knew full well I was all grown up. "Well, we better give you the tour, Jane." How did she know my name? That puzzled me for quite some time. I had no identification on me, and I never said my name. I thought maybe Jake or Mike had told them. Either way, I guess it didn't matter how she knew my name. She stood up and guided me around. "My hands," I told her. "You earn your trust," she replied. "In time, we shall remove the rope grandchild." There it was again. I couldn't help but wonder why does she keep saying that.

We headed down a dark hallway. Candles barely lighting the way. "Bathroom is down this hall. Last door on the left." She pointed up at the walls. "Our beautiful family," she explained. "Well, some ain't considered beautiful in the eyes of many, but those are weak people. They've tainted the blood of their family, thinned it out by breeding outside of what made them who they are. Even your parents plan to weaken you. They've given you no brother to grow strong with and multiply what is pure. They have lost the value of family bloodlines." Her words churned in my stomach. She knows nothing of my parents, I thought. Doesn't even know if I have a brother. We reached the end of the hallway, stopping in front of a winding staircase.

My eyes were still trying to adjust to the dim lighting as I squinted, trying to see up the stairs. "Don't be scared now Janey, I've been up and down these stairs thousands of times. I won't let you fall." She pulled on the rope leading me up the stairs. "Don't call me that." Even though I was terrified, I just couldn't allow her to call me that. She stopped to light another candle mid way up the stairway. "Call you what?" She asked, turning to me. I could see her face dimly lit by the candle on the wall. "Janey, only my mother calls me Janey." I shook as the words came out. She pulled me close to her wrinkled face. All emotions had left her eyes as they became blank. Her fingers gripped my shirt as she placed her forehead against mine. "You watch your tone, child. You live because of me. Life is what I have given to you. Be grateful, or I will have your tongue and end you where we stand." Her head slanted as she pushed me away, studying my expression. Her grip on my shirt loosened as emotion returned to her eyes. The caring grandmother she was trying to be returned as she ran her hands across my shoulders, removing the crumpled grip marks.

We reached the top of the stairs, turning into a long hallway. Maybe it was the fear, but that hallway looked as though it would stretch forever. There were three doors on this floor. One was a bathroom, which looked as though it had never been cleaned, or even used. We reached the first door on our right. Through the spacing at the bottom of the door, I could see a light flickering. "This is Mark's room. He don't like people going inside, so what say we just skip this one for now" She pulled on the rope leading me farther down the hall.

We stopped in front of the last door on the right. "This is Jeff's room. Hope you don't mind a little gore," she warned as she opened the door. She flicked a switch on the wall, filling the room with light. I couldn't believe what I was seeing. Dried skin covered the windows. Some of the walls were covered in framed body parts. One was an ear, another an eyebrow. The other walls had shelves lined with jars. Inside the jars were fingers and toes. One held a fetus stuck with pins as though it were a voodoo doll. The word 'abomination' was written across the jar. Another jar, this one much larger, held a woman's head. Her eyes were left open, forced to stare at the fetus placed next to her. I felt my stomach begin to churn. I didn't want to see anymore. "He has an unusual urge to save these things, says this is his art, a gift from the outside world. I don't see art, do you?" She asked as she pointed to a skeleton on its hands and knees forming a TV stand. "No," I replied. "All I see is insanity". She looked at me with those cold blank eyes again. "Let me show you something." She says as she moves to the closet door. She opens the door and directs me to look inside. Inside is Reen's lifeless body, hung up like he was an article of clothing. "You say insanity, but I say well taught." She slams the closet door shut and grabs the rope once more. "It's time for you to join your friends."

The caring grandmother she tried so hard to be was now gone. She was cold and spoke no words as she pulled me along.

We moved quickly down the hall once more, entering the dark staircase. I watched every step I took, trying not to trip on the way down. Finally, we reached the cellar door.

I could hear Rachel's screams as the door opened. "Down you go," she demanded. My legs shook as I began to descend the old wooden staircase. The sound of metal being sharpened filled the air. I reached the bottom to find Rachel, Jake, and Mike.

Each corner of the cellar had a small 'U' shaped wall built in front of it. In the center of the wall was a chain. They chained each of my friends to their own corner, except for Mike. He was bound to a chair. I couldn't take my eyes off of him as they led me to my corner.

The collar placed around my neck was cold and heavy; covering most of my neck. I could feel the old paint peeling off the rusted steel. An old linked chain was attached to the front of the collar. It was thick and weighed down the back of my neck. The chain wrapped around my feet, eventually entering a hole through the wall. Mark stepped from behind me and placed a large key lock on the back of the collar.

I looked around the dimly lit room at my friends. Jake had been severely beaten. One eye was completely swollen shut, the other just barely open. His neck was bruised enough to show above the collar. Blood had dried into his hands and arms. A few holes in his shirt revealed slashes on his chest. I learned quickly this was the work of Mark. As he headed for the stairs, he stopped at Jake. "Make them suffer!" He yelled as his fist pounded against Jake's chest. Out of breath, Jake collapsed on the floor. "Show them no mercy!" Mark screamed as he kicked Jake in the stomach. "Give them their pain!" Jeff yelled, stepping out from a darkened corner. He held an old meat cleaver in his right hand. He Flicked his left thumbnail over the edge of the blade as he stared at Mike. I could see the fear in Mike's eyes as Jeff stepped over to him.

Jeff pulled the chair to the center of the room. He stepped behind Mike and grabbed his chin. "Look at her," Jeff demanded, pushing Mike's head towards Rachel. "Look at her! So frail, so innocent, but soon, soon just an empty shell". He released Mike's chin and stepped in front of him. Mike couldn't stop looking at Rachel as the tears fell from his eyes. My heart raced as Jeff pulled a wooden school desk from the other side of the basement. The metal legs screeched along the ground as the desk was placed in front of Mike. Jeff pulled on a string that dangled down from a floodlight. The light flickered and swung from side to side, and we gained a much clearer vision of Jeff. His skin was wrinkled, his body was badly deformed. He had no eyebrows, and small patches of hair barely covered his head. Parts of his lips looked as though they had never fully formed, baring his teeth, which were jagged and cracked. One nostril was missing and the tip of his nose was pulled upwards. I gasped loudly at the sight. Turning to me, his teeth grinding as he moved in, leaning over me.

"Whats the matter, girl?" He asked as he pulled my hair, tilting my head back. "Do I frighten you? Or just make you sick? Look at me when I speak, girl!" He pried my eyes open and stared into them. His were blank, and cold. Almost meaningless. Both hands now gripped on my face as he spoke with his nose pressed against mine. His breath was putrid. Even now, I can still smell his rotten breath.

He stood up and began to focus his rage back on Mike. "Surely you want to be a hero, don't you, boy? Maybe save your little girlfriend over there? She looks awfully terrified in her corner. You can help her." Jeff pulled the desk closer to Mike and freed one of his hands. He pulled on Mike's arm, placing his hand on the desk, just adjacent to the meat cleaver. "All you need to do is one little thing for me, and I'll let this one go. Otherwise, she's mine. Her life will surely end, and in death, I shall enjoy what remains of her." Mike looked up at him with an agreeing look in his eyes. "I don't read minds, boy, speak up! Are you going to be a hero tonight, or do you both suffer in agony?" Jeff stepped back, waiting for an answer. "Yes" Mike replied. "Just let her be". Jeff reached for the cleaver and with joy in his voice he shouted, "I hope you're hungry, boy!" With one swift swing of the cleaver, Jeff removed four of Mike's fingers. Mike screamed as a final swing removed his thumb.

Rachel's cries filled the room as she turned away from Mike. I covered my eyes with my hands, desperately trying to avoid knowing what was going on. Covering my eyes didn't help at all. Between Jeff's demands to chew and his laughter, I could clearly hear the bones in Mike's fingers being ground between his teeth. Despite that, to make matters worse, his gags made my stomach turn. When Mike vomited, I lost it. Jeff was screaming about Mike vomiting when I fainted.

I have no idea how long I was asleep for but when I woke, Mike was still in the center of the room. His wounds had been burnt shut. An IV was inserted into his right arm, just above the wrist. Duct tape held his head against the back of the chair. A small tube came out of his neck. I had wondered what it was for. Had he stopped breathing? I thought. That question was quickly answered, however.

Jeff stepped out of the darkness with the cleaver in one hand and a blender in the other. He placed them on a small school desk and carried it to the center of the room. With a hard smack, he woke Mike from his sleep. Jeff grabbed Mike's chin and cut the tape from his head. "Don't worry, boy, you won't die today." He reassured Mike, as he turned his head from one side to the other. With a single swing, Jeff cut off Mike's hand. It looked like he tried to scream, but barely even a whisper came out. "Whats the matter, boy? Need to scream?" Jeff asked as he reached behind Mike's chair. He pulled out a small torch and started it. "I don't want you to feel left out," a smile stretched across Jeff's face as he brought the torch up to Mike's wrist. "I'll scream for you, hows that sound boy?" laughter filled the room as he sealed the wound shut. Jeff screamed as he laughed. It seamed as though he could hear the screams inside Mike's head, as though it was Jeff who was being burnt and tortured.

Eventually, the screaming stopped, and Jeff chopped Mike's hand into small pieces. He scooped them up and placed them all into the blender. He poured in water and blended it into a thick juice. Then I found out what the tube was for. Jeff placed a funnel into the tube and poured the mixture directly into Mike's stomach! I couldn't hold it anymore. I threw up. Jeff turned to me. His face was blank.

"Love it up girl, you get to watch as your friend consumes himself! Don't you just love it!"

Chapter 13

I awoke the next morning, vomit stuck to my shirt, my hair knotted. Light barely made its way through a few hopper windows. Mike was back against his wall. He hasn't woken up since Jeff gave him a dose of what he said was morphine. He said the less pain he feels, the longer he lives, which means the more he can consume. Rachel was asleep just feet away from me. Exhausted from the night before, she slept still, but far from silent. Jake knelt in the center of his wall. I don't believe he slept at all throughout the night.

I looked around the room, hoping that everything was just a nightmare. Unfortunately, the weight of the cold chain made reality sink in quickly. I tried tugging on it, even using my legs as leverage, but nothing worked. "It's useless Jane, I've tried it all, there's no way out". Jake's words made my skin crawl. I think it was the way his voice sounded with his face swollen, more than the fact that what he had said was the truth. But it was good to hear his voice. "Where is Josh?" he asked quietly. I hesitated briefly and lowered the chain to the floor. "Those two freaks mutilated him." I told him, turning towards him. "What about Reen? Have you seen him?" I looked downward and told him how the old lady took me around the house and showed me Jeff's room and his closet. "Did you tell her my name?" I hoped his answer was yes, but to my surprise, it was not. "How did you guys get here? We were bagged and thrown in the back of a truck." Jake looked towards the stairs, then moved as close to me as he could.

"We need to get out of here somehow Jane, these people, they're fucking nuts. We are all going to die. How did we get here? They dragged us. Wrapped ropes around our necks like we were cattle, then drug us all the way here. If we can get free, I know how to get back to the cemetery. Then we just take Josh's car to the main road."

The last thing I wanted was to break his spirit. Hope was all we had at the time, but I couldn't let his mind stay on one track; though it was helpful to know he could get us back to the cemetery. "No can do. We never found his car." A look of not too surprised filled his face. "That makes sense, otherwise you'd all be home right now. Poor Rachel, I never meant for this Jane, you know that, right? It was just supposed to be a little joke, that's all."

The basement door interrupted us.

The old lady walked slowly down the stairs and over to me. "Now Janey," she said in a soft voice, "I'm going to bring you upstairs, this is where the trust will be earned for you." Once more, the door opened. Chills ran down my spine as Mark entered the room. Once more, he was wielding that machete. He stepped behind Jake, grabbing his hair. Tilting his head back, he placed the blade against his neck. "No!" I screamed. "Relax, child, it is not his time yet. Merely collateral, we can call it. You fuss or give me any problem and he dies. Is this understood?" I agreed, and she began to release me from my prison. The thought of pushing her frail body down and making my way for the door heavily crossed my mind, but the thought of Jake and Rachel being slaughtered put a pit in my throat.

I stood up as she unlocked the chain around my neck. My eyes were fixed on the blade against Jake's neck. I couldn't stop looking, even as the old lady used a rope to tie my arm to hers. Before I knew it, she was pulling me along. As we climbed the stairs, the sight of Jake disappeared.

The kitchen was dimly light by a flickering light that hung above an old wooden dining table. The table was set, six places in all. The room smelt horrid. Similar to that of a rancid carcass. Over the stove was an old man stirring a large stew pot. He breathed deeply through his nose, just above the pot. Still stirring, he raised his head to look me in the eye. His right eye was cloudy. It looked as though he had been blind for some time. His hair was gray and long from the sides. On top, his balding head looked rough and riddled with scabs. "Hungry?" He asked as he tasted the food. I knew what he was cooking, though I was not sure exactly who it was. "No, and it smells disgusting," I said quickly. "She's an honest one, isn't she" he stated. "It'll grow on you soon, trust us, it's in your blood, you know."

The old lady guided me to a chair placed at the far end of the table. My legs shook violently as I sat down in the chair. She sat next to me as she rubbed my shoulder. "Listen now, child," she said as she squeezed my shoulder tightly. "This is your first time Janey, take small bites, let the meat grow on you. It's bitter and rough, but only at first. Cut the meat into small pieces and eat it with the potatoes. Too big of a piece and the tang will leave a sour taste on your tongue." My stomach churned as I watched the old man filling the bowl placed in front of me. I gagged as large chunks of at least one of my friends dropped into the bowl. Slowly, he filled the rest of the bowls, then placed bread beside each dish. The old lady screamed loudly as she stomped on the floor. Before long, the table was packed, and I could feel my bones rattle.

Chapter 14

I felt vastly out-numbered, and not to mention completely out of place. I glanced around the table as everyone crammed their mouths. Tears fell from my eyes as I tried not to think of who they might be eating. I kept reflecting on Josh, and how they were taking his organs; I kept seeing the joy in Jeff's face as he hacked limb from limb. I knew my time was running out, and I wouldn't be able to stall much longer. Eventually, I was going to have to eat. I remembered how my mother would tell me to imagine that I was the only one in the room when giving school presentations. I really didn't think that would help in this situation much, but then I remembered what my dad would always say. "Just get it over with and before you know it, it's done." That always worked for me. Except for this time. No matter what I would think, it all came down to one fact: there was human in my bowl, and I was going to have to eat it.

"Lets go, child, don't let it get cold. Food spoils that way". Her mouth was stuffed, and she chewed as she spoke. "I'm not hungry, Ma'am." I said, hoping she would let me be. "Now Jane!" The old man spoke with a stern deep voice, "I didn't slave over a hot stove so you could stare at it, you know." My father would speak those same words to me every time I didn't want to eat my vegetables. My hand shook as I reached for the fork and knife. I thought about just jamming my knife into the old lady's neck, but I knew that would just piss off Mark, and he would take it out on Jake. "Remember sweetie, small bites or you'll throw up". I looked at her and quickly said, "I'll be throwing up either way." Just get it over with, I reminded myself as I cut a small piece of meat off. I pressed the fork through the meat, then through a large piece of potato. Silence fell over the table for the first time that night as I pressed my eyes shut and put the worst tasting "food" in my mouth. Fortunately, after a few chews, my stomach couldn't handle any more. I threw up all over the table.

"Disrespectful little shit!" Mark screamed. His chair flew out from under him as he slammed his hands on the table. "Sit your ass down and watch who you're talking to," the old lady shouted back, quickly rising from her seat. "I run this house, and this family. You will mind your temper, Mark. This one is mine! Don't you forget that."

For once, I was happy she was next to me. Who knows what that man would have done to me if not for her. Unfortunately, I must have upset her. She grabbed the rope that bound us and pulled me toward the basement. "Lets go teach you some manners, little lady." I tried to gather my balance as she drug me down the stairs. "I tried to bring it out in you at dinner, but that didn't work. The outside world is deep in you. Now we do it the old-fashioned way."

She grabbed the machete from the floor and untied us. "Now, you have a choice. You can take this knife and kill your sad little friend over there. What's her name?" I didn't answer her. I couldn't even look in her eyes. She grabbed me by the shirt and pushed me against the wall, placing the blade against my neck. "I asked you a question. What's her name? Answer me, goddamn it!" Her eyes were blank as she screamed in my face. Spit splattered on my face, and I could smell the rancid meat in on her breath.

"Rachel, her name is Rachel!" She smiled briefly. "Good. You kill Rachel, or I kill your little boyfriend." She stepped back and handed me the machete. As my hand wrapped around the handle, I thought again about just killing her and freeing my friends; but I knew they were too weak to fight their way out of that place. Once again, my father's words ran through my mind. I looked at Rachel, her eyes filled with terror. Not just fear, but absolute terror. Then I looked at Mike. He was barely surviving. The surviving he was managing, I was sure it was because of the drugs. I don't think he even knew what was happening to him. Then everything went blank.

I remember waking up, once again chained to my corner. The light was still on. I tried to think about what happened. Did I actually kill her? I tried hard to remember, but with no luck. Even now, I still have no memory of what happened. I laid there on the floor for a few minutes, trying to build up the courage to look at Rachel. Finally, I pulled myself up and looked for Rachel. She wasn't there. My heart dropped to my stomach. I looked for Jake, but he was gone too. Then I saw Mike. He was right next to me, still in his chair. The machete was in his neck, about halfway through. I felt cold, and my skin grew goosebumps. I felt for my neck, no collar was there, then I found it on my leg. I couldn't figure out why they put the chain on my leg. They were testing me; I suppose. And it worked.

I knew I was going to die, and for all I knew, I was the only one left. I told Mike I was so sorry as I pulled the machete out of his neck. It took a few pulls, and his body jolted back to the chair when it finally separated. I knew I had to get out of there. Figuring out how, that was the part that took the longest.

I searched the cellar as best as I could. Searching for some sort of key. A way to remove the chain that bound me to the wall. Anything. You could call it a failure, you could call it bad luck. Whatever you want to call it, the truth was staring me in the face, but I refused to accept it.

I stared at my leg. No, I thought to myself. There had to be another way, my thoughts continuing to race. I fell to the ground, placing my head in my hands. Every thought in my mind was the same. Take the leg. Desperate times, desperate measures. I weighed my options. Leave the leg, and await the torment from my captors, or remove the leg and fight for freedom. My freedom. That's when I heard my dad's voice. As clear as if he had been standing next to me. He always told me that if a person has a chance at survival, no matter the cost, they must pay it. If not, it's no different from suicide. After a long, last glance at my leg, I came to terms with what needed to be done.

I took the machete and swung at my leg. The blade vibrated as it hit my bone. The sound made me gag as I pulled it out of my leg. Tears shot from my eyes as I swung again and again. It took three times to finally separate from my prison, and the cuts were nowhere near close to each other. After the second swing, my leg went numb. Then I looked for something to seal my leg. I knew I had to act quick or I would bleed out. I saw the furnace close by. Grabbing the machete, I crawled over and stuck it in the flame. After a few seconds, I pulled it out and pushed the blade against my cut up leg. The skin sizzled, and the pain was almost unbearable. Thankfully, adrenaline does wonders. I grabbed a broom and used the handle as a crutch. It was finally time to get out of there.

Slowly, I headed up the stairs, trying desperately not to make a sound. I twisted the knob and opened the door partially, just enough to squeeze through. Peaking around toward the kitchen, I noticed the lights were off. Looking left, I saw the front door. I headed for it, barely being able to walk. The living room was on my right. As I approached the entrance, I placed myself against the wall and peaked in.

I wish I had never looked in that living room. There was Jeff, pants on the floor, no shirt on. In front of him was a small table. On the table was Rachel's lifeless body. There was a meat cleaver in her chest, and her head had been cut almost clean off, and was hanging off the edge of the table, barely attached to her neck. There were stilts holding her legs and arms in place. A jar of vaseline was placed next to her naked body. I couldn't believe my eyes. Wasn't it enough for them to eat my friends? Now this one is having sex with my friend's dead body! I wanted to throw up. As he would thrust his hips forward, Rachel's head would flop up and down, banging onto the underside of the small table.

That was it the last straw. I crept up behind him, slowly, trying not to be heard. He was too busy to hear me hopping around. I took the machete and slammed it straight through his back. The handle hit his skin as I fell forward. I felt his body twitch under mine. I was sure he died instantly; wish I could have made him suffer, though. For everything he had done to my friends. But I told myself now I have to keep going, or I was a dead girl. I pulled myself up and made it to the front door. I opened the door as quickly as I could and practically jumped outside, where to my surprise, there was Josh's car!

I made my way over to it and fell at the driver's door. Relief building inside of me. Freedom so close, within reach. Can't stop, I thought to myself. I'm not free until I make it to Baltimore Pike. All that was left was to get inside the car and drive away. That's when I remembered Josh always had a spare key taped to the bottom of his car, just in case. I had never been happier. I pulled myself inside and started the car. It was weird driving with my left leg, but I wasn't letting it stop me.

I have no idea how I found my way back to the main road, and before I knew it, I pulled up to the hospital. I parked in the closest spot to the door. When the security guard ran over to me, I felt more safe than I have ever felt. He carried me straight into the back and was yelling for doctors. And now here I am! Alive, safe and missing a leg, but at least I'm still here. Just wish I could have found Jake. Poor Jake, heaven knows what they did to him. Hopefully, he found a way out and someone finds him, but I doubt it. He wasn't there when I left, and my only thoughts were doubtful.

"Well, while it is best to keep to positive thoughts, it may not always possible Jane," Mr. Charles tried to comfort Jane as much as he could, but it was clear, only time would help her. "Everything you went through, it's amazing that you survived. That's what's important, you know. Who knows what would have happened if you went searching for Jake. And now, your story will open the eyes of so many people, and maybe even help bring these people to justice." He told Jane as he packed up his computer.

"I know. In time, I'm sure I'll accept everything that's happened. Let's hope what you are doing gets something started soon, before some other kids wind up in that house." Jane sat up, shifting in the bed as her nurse entered the room.

With a smile on her face, she glances at the monitors. "Looks like you'll be heading on out of here first thing in the morning, Jane. Doc says today you can try walking around with your new leg, wants to take the day to get you started with therapy." She seemed more excited than Jane when she spoke. She quickly started unplugging all the monitors, humming to herself as she tucked away the cords.

Chapter 15

Most of the day was centered on getting used to the feeling of a prosthetic leg. A battery of physical therapists worked around the clock with Jane, each one focused on trying to teach her everything she would need to know as she started this alternative lifestyle. Each one reassuring her it gets easier as she progresses through therapy.

First, she started with making sure she had the right suspension system for her needs, and ensuring she knew how to secure the prosthetic correctly. She was still young, and she let them know she was planning on being quite active with the remainder of her life. This is why they suggested a dynamic vacuum system.

"Wow, okay, that's really tight. Hurts a bit. Are you sure you're not trying to cut the rest of my leg off?" Jane asked jokingly. "Of course not! Your leg is still swollen, and you most likely won't be using this until you're fully healed." He explains. "You do want the vacuum to be tight, and this is new for you. You'll become more and more comfortable with the pressure as time goes by. This system really is the most comfortable out there." He replies. "Your body weight will push any excess air out of the leg. After a few steps, everything should be set to go." Jane paid close attention to the man. "Do you see this valve over here?" He asks her. She nods just before he continues on. "That is a one-way valve. So when you first put this on, the two magnets will connect inside. They form,... like a piston. Swiveling with each step you take. Once on, you stand up and the excess air is expelled through the top, then you pull the liner over the edge and up your leg. Afterwards, with each of the first few steps, the vacuum seal is formed. That valve I showed you. It lets the air out while preventing air from entering."

Jane studies the therapist's actions closely. She's never been one to rely on someone else. Independence was important before, but now, as an amputee, she's more than determined to stand on her own. "Tell me, what kind of things can I do with this? I like going places, walking, might be awhile before I go on a hike. Given the circumstances, overnight camping is currently out of the question, but I would like to return to it. When can I try walking with this thing? I know, I am just full of questions!" Jane nervously asks what seems to be a million and one questions.

"Trust me, I completely understand. Some patients never ask these questions. Then one day we get a call, frantic because they thought they could do things and they can't. Or they can't figure out how to work it. It's always refreshing when questions are asked, no matter the amount. Now, let's try walking down the hall and back. Pay attention to how it feels when you're walking and remember, eventually it won't be so uncomfortable, or awkward. Then we'll take the leg off, and you can try it by yourself, Jane." She looks at him with a quirky smile, "I really don't think I need to practice taking the leg off, I have done that once already, pretty sure I got the hang of it, what do you think I'm doing here!" Jane says with a quirky smile across her face. She hides her frustration and pain well.

Several more would follow as the day progressed. Barely leaving her anytime to just relax. There was one for just walking, one for climbing stairs, even one for sitting down and standing up. Around three in the afternoon, Jane locked herself in the bathroom.

"It's never going to stop," she thought to herself. She listened through the bathroom walls as doctors went in and out of her neighbor's room. She tried hard to understand what was being said, even just a name. Unfortunately, their voices were mumbled. She felt horrible for the poor soul, and worse every time the alarms went off in his room. The doctors would rush in, codes over the loudspeakers would be yelled and then everything would die down, leaving an eerie calm cast over the atmosphere. She contemplated going next door to talk to him, let him know he was not alone and whatever had happened to him was now over, even though she knew he wouldn't respond. Then, she heard a familiar voice calling in to her room.

"Jane! Jane, are you in here, hun?" A female voice called out to her. "Hold on, just one second," Jane replied as she pulled herself to her feet. Stepping out of the bathroom, her heart stopped. Rachel's mother had come to pay her a visit. "Oh dear, look what they did to you!" She cried as she rushed over to Jane, wrapping her arms around her. "I'm so sorry about Rachel. I tried so hard to look after her the...."

"Now Jane," she interrupted, "don't you worry about that. There was nothing you could do. One day we can sit down and talk about all this, but today I'm here to tell you not to worry about any of that. We are all saddened by this tragedy, and all thankful that at least you survived." She sat down with Jane and explained how her parents had been visiting everyone since their return.

"Nobody is pointing at you, Jane. We don't want you to worry anymore about this. The police have been searching all the way to Brandywine, and Delaware police have taken over the search from there. Nothing has been found yet. I thought it would be best if I came and let you know that the search is coming to an end. Just like all those years ago, history repeats itself, hunny, and that's precisely what is happening now. And just like back then, the case will go cold, unless maybe when you are feeling better if you remember how to get there, you might take a cop out there, but that is only up to you; no one else. And Jane, none of us will ask you to do that." Her voice was reassuring and somewhat comforting. Her visit lasted about an hour, which Jane was thankful for every minute, especially since no doctors, nurses or physical therapists would snatch her away while she had a visitor.

Dinner had arrived just after the doctor paid his last visit. He made sure Jane was familiar with her new leg and comfortable walking with it. Then told her he'll see her just before they discharged her in the morning. He clarified that he wanted to see her to the front door, and how proud of her he was. Jane had asked if it would be okay if she said a few words to the man next door as the doctor was leaving. "I think it would be best if you worried about eating, then if you still want to, sure. You never know, it may do him some good!" She nodded and pulled the tray closer, removing the lid. "Yuck, green beans!"

The sound of the emergency alarms grabbed Jane's attention. An all too familiar sound of the heart monitor flat lining echoed out from the room next door. She leaned forward in her bed and watched as the nurses rushed to her neighbor's room. Jane couldn't help but feel more and more sorry for the guy. Since his arrival, the doctors have rushed to his room more times than she cared to count for. Today alone, this was the third time. This time was different. She made her way to her door to hear a conversation from two of the nurses. Neither one had a clue what was wrong with him, and Jane was thinking that none of the doctors did either. She could hear the defibrillators charging, again and again. The uncertainty in the doctor's voice was clear every time he said, "Come on, Son, don't give up," a brief pause then "Clear." She heard that word three times before a long pause. Her eyes filled with tears as she heard another doctor's voice call out, "Okay, that's enough. Time to call it"

The tears ran fast down past her cheek. She couldn't quite understand why. Maybe it was because she had experienced something so similar to what this person had gone through. Maybe it was because she had listened to all the times he had pulled through and found hope that he would survive. Her legs felt weak as she listened to a nurse call out "9:30-" but before she could finish, the sound of a loud scream interrupted her. The beeping of the heart monitor followed. For the first time in days, Jane found herself smiling. A genuine smile. Something she had not truly done since Jake was complimenting her at the party.

"Can you hear me, Son?" the doctor spoke in a deep and relieved voice. "Do you know where you are? Can you tell me your name?" He asked. Jane was so overwhelmed by excitement that she finally decided she was going to head over and meet her neighbor once and for all. First she had to wait till everything calmed down, then she would head over. She did not care if he was awake or sleeping. Maybe just someone telling him he's not alone would help, she thought.

Fifteen minutes after the doctors and nurses left his room, she made her way over to him. She leaned her head out of her door to see if anyone was around. She looked down both ways of the hallway. Everything was clear. Not a nurse in sight. She began to get nervous as she made her way next door. Slowly, she opened the door. As she entered the room, she allowed her eyes to gaze around. There were no personal belongings, no family members, grieving or otherwise. Slowly she passes the bathroom located to the right of her, coming up to a curtain that was pulled completely around the bed. She pauses, building the courage to open the curtain and say what she came to say. Hands shaking, she reached for the curtain, opening it while trying not to wake her neighbor. Her eyes widened, her arms gave way, her voice echoed through-out the hospital floor. She fell to ground as she yelled out "Jake!"

The loud thud of her body smacking against the floor and her voice caused the nurses to run to her. One of them helped her to her feet, trying to get her to return to her room. "NO!" she insisted. "It's Jake, I have to see him, I have to see him now!" She made her way to his bed, pulling a chair alongside. She grabbed his hand and kissed his forehead. Looking around, she realized there was no way for her to curl up next to him, so she sat on the chair and placed her head on his chest. "I'm so sorry," she cried as she repeated herself. "I'm so sorry".

The sound of her dad's voice woke Jane. She found herself still next to Jake, her hand firmly placed in his. She lifted her head, ready to call out for her parents, when she heard her father, fully enraged. "No, I will not calm down!" he yelled. "We are Beans by blood, regardless of our actions. They have broken family law, and for that, we deal with our own!"

Also by Jimi Peranteau

Welcome To Satanville
Leg of Jane
Bloodlines

Watch for more at https://www.amazon.com/author/jimperanteau_13.

About the Author

Jimi Peranteau is a 39 year old husband, father, multi-musician, truck driver, and extreme horror author. His novella series Welcome to Satanville has two entrees, Leg of Jane and Bloodlines.

He is currently writing his next work of fiction titled Mason's Jars, which is a serial killer thriller novel about 15 year veteran FBI agent Richard Wesling and his team as they hunt down a successful, vicious killer who's taunting the country with the stories of his victims. Tired of the same old routine Mason is looking for one final thrill, and he's using the nation and Agent Wesling to get it.

Follow Jimi Peranteau on Facebook https://www.facebook.com/ horrorauthor.books?mibextid=ZbWKwL

Follow Jimi Peranteau on Instagram jim.peranteau_author

Follow Jimi Peranteau on TikTok horrorauthor_jperanteau

Read more at https://www.amazon.com/author/ jimperanteau_13.

www.ingramcontent.com/pod-product-compliance
Lightning Source LLC
Chambersburg PA
CBHW051433150726
48000CB00005B/2088